NEW HAVEN FREE PUB LIB

3 5000 03522 4483

JUN 3 1 1997

NOV 3 1984

APR 21 2001

FEB 17 2004

DEC 28 2006 FREE PUBLIC LIBRARY
NEW HAVEN, CONN.

AUG 07 2008

FEB 05 2013

D1569019

OFFICIALLY WITHDRAWN
NEW HAVEN FREE PUBLIC LIBRARY

MAR 21 2024

The House on Quai Notre Dame

Georges Simenon

The House on Quai Notre Dame

Translated by Alastair Hamilton

A Helen and Kurt Wolff Book

Harcourt Brace Jovanovich

New York and London

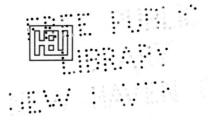
FREE PUBLIC LIBRARY NEW HAVEN

Copyright © 1962 by Georges Simenon
English translation copyright © 1975 by Georges Simenon

All rights reserved. No part of this publication
may be reproduced or transmitted in any form or
by any means, electronic or mechanical, including
photocopy, recording, or any information storage
and retrieval system, without permission in
writing from the publisher.

Printed in the United States of America

Library of Congress Cataloging in Publication Data

Simenon, Georges, 1903–
  The house on Quai Notre Dame.

  Translation of Les autres.
  "A Helen and Kurt Wolff book."
  I. Title.
PZ3.S5892Ho3   [PQ2637.I53]   843'.9'12   75–9682
ISBN 0-15-142181-1

First edition

B C D E

The House on Quai Notre Dame

Uncle Antoine died on Tuesday, on Halloween, probably at about eleven o'clock in the evening. That same night Colette tried to throw herself out of the window.

At more or less the same time, we heard that Edouard was back and that several people had seen him in town.

All this caused a considerable stir in the family, and all the members assembled for the first time in years at the funeral yesterday.

Now, on Sunday evening, it is still raining. The shutters and the windowpanes are being buffeted by gusts of wind and I can hear the interminable flow of water from the gutter a yard away from my window. In the park behind the railings, known as the Botanical Garden, the trees are stooping and broken branches mingle with the dead leaves in the avenues.

From time to time a car drives down our road, raising a spray of dirty water, but there are no pedestrians. If I pull back the curtain I can see the urinal just under my window, against the railings. Beyond the park I can see the tops of the pillars and the roof of the law courts and, farther off, in the orange-colored light emanating from the center of the town, the two towers of the cathedral.

Movie houses and restaurants are open for the night. Couples are hugging close to the buildings, and a number of umbrellas have undoubtedly been turned inside out.

I spent some time at the window before I started writing, watching the landscape distorted by the water that pours down the panes. Then I drew the curtain and put two logs in the grate.

It is all very like that evening three years ago, at the same time of year, when it had been raining and I tried to write my story, or, rather, our story, the story of my wife and myself, but more of myself, of course, since I was the one who was writing it.

In one month I wrote the length of a novel and, in my mind, it was indeed a novel, in every way as exciting as those invented by proper writers, with the advantage of being true from beginning to end. When it was finished, I admit that I wanted it to be published, if only to show certain people that I am not altogether ineffectual.

First, I sent it to a publisher in Paris, who returned it to me a few weeks later with the same polite letter that he probably sends to all the authors he turns down.

I then thought about a novelist, all of whose books I read and with whose characters I can identify. Of all the authors I know, he is the only one whose characters seem to me to be men like myself, with the same problems, the same worries, the same reactions.

I told myself that that man, who is not very much older than I, would understand me, and I sent him my manuscript together with a letter in which I explained to him, a little awkwardly perhaps, why I had decided to turn to him.

Contrary to my expectations, he replied within the week. I now regret the moment of fury when I tore his letter into little pieces and threw them into the fire. I thought that every one of his sentences was engraved in my memory, but now that I want to quote them, I cannot reconstruct them. I burned the manuscript, too, and I had tears in my eyes when I saw the sheets burst into flame among the logs.

What exactly did he say to me and what was it about his letter that left me with such a sense of bitterness? Is that the right word? Was it not that I felt humiliated, as though I had been caught in a degrading posture?

Of course he "read me from beginning to end with great interest." He added that it was "a human document" and he used the word "moving" in the same sentence. But, precisely because of that, he "didn't feel that it was a work of literature in the true sense of the term."

He didn't use the word "confession," but I felt that it was at the back of his mind.

"I think I am right in saying that you can be identified with your character and that you yourself experienced fairly recently . . ."

I made no attempt to hide the fact. If the book had been published, a number of people would not have failed to recognize me. So why did I feel so hurt? Because of that sentence, which I cannot recall completely, a sentence both explicit and reticent to which he must have given considerable thought, writer that he is.

"As I read you, I had the rather unpleasant impression that I was watching reluctantly . . ."

What do the words matter? I understood. He felt, he told me, that he was becoming a sort of voyeur, a man who enjoys observing the somewhat sordid activities of his neighbors.

In other words, I was no more or less than an exhibitionist.

It was, as I said, our story, the story of Irène and myself. I didn't hide anything. I'm not ashamed of anything. I may very well come back to it, but this time, because of Uncle Antoine's death, Edouard's extraordinary return, and all that has happened in these past few days, my story will have a less personal touch and it will no longer be possible to compare me to certain individuals whom I sometimes see looming out of the urinal at night as a young maidservant walks past.

I will no doubt be accused of sullying the name of the Huets, of washing our dirty linen in public. But I don't care. Enough people have assumed the right to take an interest in me for me to have the right to take an interest in others.

My wife is reading in bed, unaware that I am writing.

From time to time I can hear her turning the page, because the door is ajar. She will soon be asking me, without raising her voice:

"What are you doing?"

And I shall answer as usual:

"Nothing."

She won't go on about it. She'll light another cigarette, turn over some more pages, then look at the clock and mutter:

"Aren't you going to bed?"

"Right away . . ."

Just in time to slip the sheets into a drawing pad where I keep some old sketches and which nobody, least of all Irène, would ever dream of opening.

Tuesday evening, Halloween, we were supposed to dine at home with Nicolas Macherin, whom we both call Nic despite the difference of age. Toward the end of the afternoon he telephoned from Paris, where he had to spend a few days on business, and told my wife that he would be coming back on the night train.

So we dined on our own and Adèle, the maid, who wanted to go out, accelerated the meal. We ended up by going to the movies. Irène took the car out of the garage while I waited on the sidewalk, and she drove, as she always does, which is perfectly natural, since it's her car.

Because of the one-way streets, we passed by the Grand Théâtre, lighted up as if for a gala performance, and I noticed that the people getting out of their cars in front of the portico were in evening dress. I didn't realize at the time that a concert was being performed and, above all, that Colette was there, accompanied by Jean Floriau.

We finally reached the Rialto, which was in existence

in my youth and which had been modernized since. On our way back we walked all the way down Rue de la Cathédrale and then down Rue des Chartreux. Even though it had not started to rain, there was a dampness in the air, which made the lights less sharp and gave them a slightly mysterious quality.

"Shall we have a drink?" I suggested.

"If you like . . ."

We were in front of the Café Moderne, a bustling place humming with voices, and I saw some more people in dinner jackets and two or three acquaintances. Irène examined the faces around her myopically, in the hope (I realized) of finding some friends with whom we could prolong the evening. For she hates going home early once she is out.

At midnight, however, we both got up to fetch the car, which was parked in front of the cathedral.

I can't remember what we said to one another. We didn't talk very much—we very rarely have a real conversation—and I again waited on the sidewalk while she put the car back in the garage.

It was purely by chance that we didn't pass by Quai Notre Dame on our way home, as we do so frequently. Although the embankment is very close to the center of town and is virtually part of it, it is an area of darkness and silence.

Next to the dark hulk of the bishop's palace, where there are never more than two or three lights on in the windows, is a garden surrounded by high walls, and then some private houses with carriage gateways built at the beginning of the last century. The third house, of gray stone and one of the largest, belonged to my uncle Antoine and I can still remember the impression that huge building made on me when I was a child and my mother said to me as we went by:

"That's where your uncle Antoine lives."

Even later, when I went there regularly, in so far as any of us ever went there regularly, I was impressed by the solemnity of Quai Notre Dame, by its arrogant and aloof display of wealth.

We live in a modern part of town that has become one of the most fashionable areas. Our neighbors are successful doctors and lawyers, and important industrialists. Day and night, resplendent cars are parked along the sidewalk. In a certain sense, all that is part of what life is about and it is perfectly possible to imagine what goes on at night behind the curtains, how people behave, what they say at table. It never comes as a surprise to recognize them at the movies or in a café.

Maybe because of my childhood memories, I can hardly visualize anyone living on Quai Notre Dame going to the movies. Sometimes, at night, a pair of curtains remains open and one can glimpse, in a subdued light, a ceiling with heavy moldings and walls that are garnet-colored or covered with paneling. Only rarely does one see the outlines of a human being, and then, almost invariably, it is that of a motionless old man.

What would have happened if we had driven down

Quai Notre Dame that evening on our way home? I would certainly have glanced automatically at my uncle's house. Was there a light on at midnight? Had Colette already come back? Was Jean Floriau's car still in front of the door? Was there anything outside the building to suggest that something tragic has just taken place and that a further dramatic incident was about to end less tragically?

I can still see us in our room, undressing. As I watched Irène take off her stockings, I wanted to make love to her, but then I thought that she had been in such a bad mood all evening and that she would simply assume a resigned expression, so I gave up the idea.

"Good night."

"Good night."

"Are you going to the cemetery tomorrow morning?"

"If it's not raining too hard."

My wife doesn't go to the cemetery on All Souls' Day, although her mother is buried there. She never talks about her father, who died, admittedly, when she was only about ten years old. She still has some aunts and cousins in town, in the Grand-Vert district, over by the shipyards and the factories, but she has broken the ties with her family once and for all. She lives as though she had neither a childhood nor a youth. She never says:

"When I was little . . ."

Or even:

"I had an uncle who . . ."

All that aspect of her past has been crossed out, blotted out, probably because it was too squalid. She has turned into another person, who has nothing to do with the Taboués and the Loiseaus who procreated her.

I haven't been to Mass since I was fifteen, to the despair of my mother, who goes every morning and who has her own prayer stool in church. But I have remained true to certain traditions, like going to the cemetery the morning of Allhallows or All Souls' Day.

I wanted to leave early in the morning because Nicolas Macherin would undoubtedly be lunching with us. When I got up noiselessly and went into the dining room in my dressing gown, the wind had started blowing and there was a low sky with huge rain clouds lying in wait. Some people with their hands in their pockets were walking rapidly down the avenue, which cuts diagonally across the Botanical Garden.

I had just had a bath and shave when I was surprised to hear the front-door bell ring. We rarely receive unexpected visits, especially the morning of Allhallows, and I opened the bathroom door a fraction to make sure that Adèle had gone to see who it was.

My surprise was still greater when I recognized the voice of my mother, who hadn't set foot in our house for over three years—in other words, since we've been seeing Nicolas and people have been gossiping about us. I've gone on visiting her in her own house, without Irène, of course, and she has tried to cross-question me on several occasions.

"Tell me, Blaise, don't you think it may damage you in the long run?"

When she says that, I always take on an innocent

expression, because it's a subject that I can't discuss with her. She would be the last person to understand.

"Damage me?"

"Some people say that there has already been talk of your losing your job at the Academy of Arts."

"Let them talk."

"I don't understand. If only you knew how miserable it makes me! When I think of your father, so high principled and scrupulous, who would never have accepted a penny from anyone . . ."

Yet it was my mother who rang my front-door bell on the morning of Allhallows and who waited in the living room while I hurriedly got dressed.

"What is it?" asked a sleepy voice in the semi-obscurity of the bedroom.

I answered Irène:

"My mother. I don't know why she's here."

I found her in full rig, all dressed in black with what seemed to me a slight smell of incense coming from her clothes. Her eyes were red. She was sniffling, her handkerchief in her hand.

"Haven't you heard the news yet?" she asked me, rather suspiciously.

"What news?"

Her eyes focused on the telephone.

"But you've got a telephone, haven't you?"

My mother didn't, and obstinately refused to have one installed.

"I wonder why they didn't tell you."

"Who?"

"Your cousin Jean could have telephoned or, if he's too busy, he could have got his wife to call . . ."

She meant Floriau, my cousin Monique's husband, who, at the age of thirty-eight, is a distinguished heart specialist.

"Your uncle Antoine is dead . . . I'm sure they've told everybody except you."

She looked around uneasily, as though she were afraid of seeing my wife appear, and asked in a whisper:

"Where is she?"

"She's asleep."

"Are you sure she's not going to get up?"

"Not within the next hour, that's for sure. Sit down."

My mother remained standing. So did I. Despite the news she had given me, she found the time to scan the living room with a critical, not to say a shocked, expression. And I knew it wasn't the modernity that shocked her. She was working out the value of the carpets, the upholstery, the pictures. I was sure she was thinking, It's not on a drawing-teacher's salary that . . .

I wonder if I wasn't more distressed than she was by the news she brought. Like the other members of the Huet family, I only saw my uncle very seldom in his house on Quai Notre Dame. I always found him standing with his back to the fire in his book-lined study with its high ceiling. His thick glasses gave him a slightly ingenuous expression.

He was too polite ever to seem surprised at our visits. He looked as though he regarded them as perfectly normal, and he would point to an armchair in front of him.

"How is your wife? How are you?"

At the age of seventy-two he was just as alert, his mind was just as sharp, as if he were in his prime. His body was short, squat, thickset, and, since he was always bent, he made me think of a gorilla.

That brings to my mind something my mother said one day as we were leaving his house:

"How terrible to be so ugly!"

Admittedly, she had added immediately:

"But he's so intelligent!"

Uncle Antoine, the last male survivor of his generation of the Huet family, was really ugly. His face, wider than it was long, was that of certain Mongols one sees at the movies who always play the traitor parts. In its center, almost drowned in the soft flesh of the cheeks, was a ridiculously small and squashed nose.

"Who told you the news?" I asked my mother. "When did it happen?"

"Yesterday evening . . . nobody knows exactly at what time. This morning I went to Sainte-Barbe thinking that I'd be halfway to the cemetery. On my way out I met Monique and her two children . . ."

As I said, Monique is my cousin who married Jean Floriau, the doctor. They have two daughters aged eight and twelve.

"You know that Monique didn't sleep all night?

Yesterday evening her husband went out with Colette . . ."

Colette is Uncle Antoine's wife. She's thirty-one years younger than he is, and, just from the way my mother uttered her name, it was possible to infer a whole mass of unexpressed thoughts.

"They're both very good friends, you knew that?"

I was well aware that Floriau went more frequently to the house on Quai Notre Dame than any other member of the family.

"Monique only thinks about her children and nearly always refuses to go out in the evenings. Antoine never goes out. So when there's a play or a concert on, Floriau often accompanies Colette."

My mother watched my reactions, perhaps establishing a similarity between this situation and my own marriage.

"I always said she was mad . . ."

"Colette?"

"Hysterical, in any case . . . I know what I know . . . . It doesn't matter. This is no time to talk about it and, besides, it would take too long."

She was still looking at the door, unable to forget my wife's invisible presence in the apartment.

"To cut a long story short, Colette and Floriau went to the concert together yesterday evening. Your uncle Antoine stayed at home with François and appears to have gone to bed about half past nine . . ."

I have always known François at the house on Quai Notre Dame and I could swear that he hasn't changed since

I was a child. Chauffeur, butler, and valet all in one, it is he who hires the other servants and gives them their orders, for Colette takes no notice of the household.

"After making sure that your uncle didn't need anything, François went to bed on the third floor and didn't hear a thing. Toward midnight Floriau drove Colette home. Seeing that all the lights were out, he didn't go in and drove off the minute he saw the door close.

"Monique waited for her husband at home because she never goes to bed before he does. The children were asleep. She started when she heard the telephone and at first she thought it was a patient or the hospital. She hardly recognized Colette's voice. She spoke as though she were hallucinating, hardly knowing what she was saying.

" 'Help!' she shouted. 'He's dead . . .'

"You can imagine how Monique felt, since her husband hadn't come back yet.

" 'Where are you? What's happened?'

" 'I'm at home. I found him dead in his bed . . .'

" 'Uncle Antoine?'

" 'Jean must come at once. I don't know . . . I'm frightened . . .'

" 'How about François?'

" 'What about François?'

" 'Isn't he at home?'

" 'I don't know. I haven't seen him. I haven't seen anyone. I'm all alone . . . I'm frightened . . . It's terrible. . . .'

" 'Ring for François. I'm sure he hasn't gone out.'

" 'I'll try, yes. But I wish Jean would come right away
. . . there might still be a chance.'

" 'You mean he isn't dead?'

" 'I don't know . . . I think so . . . Yes . . .' "

According to my mother, who heard it from Monique,
Colette didn't even replace the receiver and left it hanging
from the telephone.

Monique waited for her husband on the doorstep.
When she saw the headlights of his car she rushed down.

Floriau, still in his dinner jacket underneath his
overcoat, turned straight back.

"We must go there, Blaise," said my mother impa-
tiently. "Go and inform your wife . . ."

She was still afraid of finding herself face to face with
Irène.

"I'll tell you the rest of the story on the way."

But just as I was getting up she managed to give me
another piece of news.

"They say disasters never come singly . . . You know
who's in town and has apparently been here for several
days? Your cousin Edouard! What can that mean? And
what's going to happen now?"

Each of these words became dramatic in my mother's
mouth, for she has an unfailing sense for catastrophes.

"I'll be along at once . . ."

I found Irène sitting in bed finishing her breakfast. She
looked at me questioningly.

"Uncle Antoine is dead," I said, and I couldn't help
panting slightly, like my mother.

My wife gazed at me in surprise, a piece of toast in her hand.

"He was over seventy, wasn't he?"

"Seventy-two or seventy-three, I don't quite know which."

"Didn't he have a weak heart?"

"Like all the Huets. But he buried the rest of them, all the same."

"Are you going over there? Will you be back for lunch?"

"I don't know."

She leaned toward me and I kissed her vaguely on the forehead. I suddenly realized that in my mind or, rather, in my subconscious, Uncle Antoine had never really been like other men. And I was sure this wasn't merely because his death was the death of a generation, my father's generation.

I remember that in that moment an idea struck me but I did not have time to elaborate. My cousin Edouard, who had just mysteriously reappeared in town, was now the oldest member of the family. He was forty-one, a year older than I and four years older than my brother, Lucien.

When I saw my mother again, I asked her:

"Does Lucien know?"

"He must have heard the news at the paper . . ."

For my brother is a subeditor at *Le Nouvelliste*.

"Come along, Blaise."

I took my coat, joined my mother in the elevator, and went toward the garage. She followed me with short, quick steps, because she's not much bigger than Uncle Antoine.

"Do you think it'll take too long on foot?"

As I stood next to the car, which was a very feminine light-blue color, I searched feverishly in my pockets.

"I left the keys upstairs," I admitted.

"Let's walk, Blaise . . . I assure you that I would rather."

For she felt that the car didn't belong to me but to my wife!

We crossed the park, leaning forward against the squalls of wind, and my mother had to shout to make herself heard.

"You know Floriau. He's a cold, controlled, and meticulous man. They say he's a great doctor, but there are plenty of others who aren't half as pompous . . . He found Antoine dead in his bed and, as soon as she heard him coming up the stairs, Colette had thrown herself onto the body raving. It appears that the cook is on vacation and that the only woman in the house was a rather stupid sixteen-year-old maid . . .

"Your cousin had to start off by looking after Colette. He had to drag her into her room, where she was undressed and put to bed. He gave her an injection to tranquilize her . . . It can't have been strong enough, for just when Floriau was calling his wife from the next room to tell her what was going on, he heard a ghastly din and screams of terror.

"When he rushed next door he found Colette, who had thrown the windows wide open and broken a pane in the process, trying to jump into the street while the little maid clung to her.

"I don't know whether it was an act . . . it might have been. Even lunatics put on acts, and when she was young she wanted to be an actress . . . she even went to drama school."

"Who told you that?"

"She did, one day when your uncle asked me to have tea with her because she was feeling depressed . . ."

We crossed the park leaving the gray pillars of the law courts on our left, and went toward the Pont Vieux, where the passers-by walked bent over, holding on to their hats in the storm.

"You can imagine what Monique must have been through! This was the second time she was cut off in the middle of a telephone conversation. When her husband called a few minutes later, he asked her to get in touch with the hospital on his behalf and get them to send him a nurse immediately . . .

"He didn't come home to change until six o'clock in the morning . . ."

I didn't ask my mother what my uncle died of, so sure was I of the answer. His father, Jules Huet, the founder of the family, had died of a heart attack when he was about fifty-four, the day after the armistice in 1918. His second son, Fabien, the father of Edouard the black sheep and of Monique the doctor's wife, had suffered from angina pectoris for five years and finally succumbed to it when he was forty-five. As for my father, the third of the Huet sons, he collapsed in his architectural studio the day before his fiftieth birthday.

Now that Antoine had died, the only remaining member of that generation was a daughter, Juliette, who must be about sixty, and who, ever since she became a widow, had run a carrier company in the northern outskirts of the town. She was now called Lemoine. She had children and grandchildren, whom I hardly knew by sight, as though they were a stray branch of the family.

We were going past the façades of the vast patrician houses when my mother suddenly seized me by the arm.

"I wonder if we're still in time to speak to your cousin Floriau . . . At six o'clock this morning he had told only his wife about it, but I suppose the coroner must have been since . . ."

I looked at her in surprise in the cold, in the north wind that had turned her face blue, and then she let go of my arm and looked around to make sure that nobody was listening:

"According to Floriau, Antoine didn't die a natural death . . . he poisoned himself. . . ."

I pressed the button sunk in the middle of a heavy bronze rosette and my mother and I waited outside the carriage door, listening with awe to the silence of the house. My fingers were tingling in spite of my gloves, and my nostrils and eyelids were moist.

When a window opened, we both looked up at the same time. But it was a window in the house next door and an old woman stood there motionless, observing us with an expressionless face. Did she know already? A door opened within. We heard footsteps on the paving stones beneath the archway. The small door cut into the main entrance opened slightly, and was then pulled back far enough to let us in.

"How terrible, François!"

For the first time in my life I realized that the butler was older than my uncle. I wouldn't be surprised if he were nearly eighty. He was clean-shaven, dressed in black as usual, with a four-in-hand tie of immaculate white, hardly

whiter, however, than his tired face, whose features pro-
truded with the exaggeration of a caricature.

He didn't reply to my mother, simply nodded. The
archway led to a glazed door that gave onto a large paved
courtyard with a row of erstwhile stables at the far end and
an enormous lime tree in the middle.

We went through another glazed door opening onto a
hall reached by seven or eight white marble steps. One of
the doors on the ground floor was open but the shutters
inside the room were closed and, in the gloom, all that
could be seen was the light reflected in the moldings of the
furniture.

I knew this ground floor because, as a child, I had
pried about in the rooms while my parents chatted in my
uncle's study. There are nothing but drawing rooms, two
large ones and one smaller one, dark by day, with, on the
walls, some old portraits, landscapes with gilded frames,
and, in the first drawing room, an ancient tapestry covering
an entire wall with a hunting scene.

The hall alone is two or three times as big as our living
room, paved with such a smooth and polished white marble
that there is a permanent danger of measuring one's length
on it. Two balusters support bronze negroes brandishing
torches, and a double staircase, covered by a thick, garnet-
colored carpet, leads up to the first floor.

There was a sense of total emptiness and an extraordinary immobility in the air, a total absence of vibrations,
noises, and smells. The only other places that have ever
given me that impression are museums.

And it wasn't because of my uncle's death. I have always remembered the house on Quai Notre Dame as neutral and inhuman, except for the study, where life and heat appeared to be concentrated.

We were never really welcomed to the house, my father, my mother, and I, and I don't think that any member of the family, except perhaps Jean Floriau—and even here I'm not so sure—was ever invited to a meal.

We would call on my uncle. On some occasions I saw my father being offered a glass of port and a cigar, but in most cases it was tea and dry cakes, completely different from any cakes I have eaten elsewhere.

And yet the drawing rooms on the ground floor, with their stiff chairs covered in damask and brocade, had served a purpose. So had the large dining room on the first floor. I can't imagine those dinners or those parties. I know the names of some of the guests, solemn, distinguished men, French or foreign bankers, politicians, or even heads of state of small countries, who required my uncle's advice.

We all went up to the second floor in silence, and, without a word, François opened the door and my mother made a couple of hesitant steps before stopping dead and crossing herself.

Antoine Huet had been laid on his bed, in the traditional manner of the dead, his hands crossed on his chest. The curtains had not been drawn or the candles lighted, and it was the cold, gray light of day that illuminated the room and the body. I realized that that shocked my mother and that she was looking for someone.

Floriau came out of the next room, dressed in gray, his face gray, too, for lack of sleep.

"My God, Jean!"

He looked at her with his clear eyes, which expressed nothing other than a slight impatience.

"Who told you, Aunt?"

"Your wife. I met her as I was coming out of church and she told me everything. My God, Jean! Why don't you draw the curtains? This isn't like a room where somebody has just died." She added with a touch of spite, knowing that Floriau was not a practicing Catholic:

"He hasn't even got a rosary in his hands! I'm going to give him mine . . ."

"It's not worth it, Aunt."

"Why? What do you mean?"

"They're coming for him."

"Coming for him?"

"Try and keep calm. It's complicated enough as it is. I'm expecting the police inspector at any moment. The coroner came a few minutes ago and agrees with me."

"Did you really have to tell him?"

"Yes, I did. It's too complicated to explain. I'm a doctor and I have no right . . ."

"Are you sure you're not mistaken?"

"Certain."

His voice had become abrupt.

"What's going to happen to him?"

"He'll be taken to the morgue for an autopsy."

"Are you taking care of that?"

She had become harsh, too, almost threatening, as though it were she, who was only a Huet by marriage, who had to defend the honor of the family.

"No. The medical expert. That's the rule in case of suicide."

"Even for a man like him, with such important connections?"

I noticed on his bed table a half-empty glass of water, a pair of spectacles, and a bottle that still contained a few white tablets.

"Why would he have done something like that, Jean? He had everything he wanted . . ."

My mother revealed what was at the back of her mind by adding bluntly:

"How's Colette? Your wife told me . . ."

"She had a second attack when she came to . . . I had to give her another injection. She's got a nurse with her and she'll be taken to the Saint Joseph Nursing Home shortly."

"Poor woman!"

My mother loathed her, but she was talking to Floriau, who was said to be Colette's lover. Or so it was rumored in the family.

My mother didn't like Floriau, either; but she felt a certain respect for him because he was a well-known doctor whom people spoke of as a future professor, and also because it was impossible to break through his icy calmness.

"Don't you think she's always been slightly mad? I heard that her mother died in an asylum in the south . . ."

She didn't add the words on the tip of her tongue: ". . . and that Antoine was paying the expenses."

She preferred to change the subject once more. Drawing nearer to the bed, she remarked:

"He's almost handsome!"

It was true. Death had removed from my uncle's face a babyish, incongruous quality, and it now appeared extraordinarily serene. I even thought I could perceive a smile at the corners of his lips, which I had never seen when he was alive.

"Didn't he leave a letter or anything? Can you understand why he went like that, without a word to anybody?"

The next sentence made me suspicious, because everything counts with my mother, every word, every intonation, every silence.

"You know that Edouard has been in town for some days, don't you? I don't know if he's been to see his wife and child, but I'd be astonished if he had. Although it appears that his wife was stupid enough to send him some money on several occasions . . ."

Could Floriau see what was coming, too? It didn't look like it. He listened politely, but he also seemed to be waiting uneasily for something, the arrival of the police inspector, no doubt. He must have resented his wife's having talked to my mother at this indeterminate stage of the proceedings.

"What would you do if he turned up?"

I now knew why my mother had come to see me so

early in the morning, at my house, with the risk of meeting Irène.

Of course, Floriau had been the first man on the spot. He was there by chance, because he had gone out with Colette that evening and when she found her husband dead she had naturally telephoned him. He had taken everything in hand immediately. Had he not just spoken as though it were solely up to him whether my aunt was to be sent to a nursing home or not?

What soon transpired from my mother's words was that Floriau was not a Huet. And even if he had been, he would not have been the oldest of the living Huets.

The eldest was this Edouard who had just reappeared in town in an inexplicable and disquieting manner.

My mother first put the question to Floriau, who appeared, for the time being, at least, as the master of the house.

"What would you do if he turned up?"

But she didn't give him time to answer and turned toward me.

"And what do you think about it, Blaise? After Edouard you're the eldest . . ."

Hadn't Uncle Antoine sworn to his mother on her deathbed that his fortune would go to the Huets whatever happened? This was in 1948, in this same house where, at the time, Colette had not yet set foot, and it had seemed that she would never do so.

Antoinette Huet had been eighty-one, her son fifty.

I was thirty years old at the time and, like the rest of

the family, I went to the funeral. Everybody looked for Colette, whom they knew about, wondering whether she would dare to appear. She did not. Antoine, overwhelmed with grief, had hardly talked to anybody.

Since that day, everybody repeated the solemn promise he had made to his dying mother. What did they know about it? Nobody had been present during that last conversation.

Yet, ever since, they had repeated with the greatest assurance, even after Antoine's marriage:

"One day we'll inherit."

My mother was sure. Aunt Sophie, the widow of my uncle Fabien, the mother of Edouard and Monique, and almost seventy-nine, shared this conviction.

Had my mother not come to Uncle Antoine's house that morning in order to keep an eye on her inheritance? And had she not brought me as a means of support, since I, at least, was a genuine Huet?

From the half-open door of the next room came a groan and my mother asked:

"Is she in pain, Jean?"

He replied condescendingly, like a doctor reluctant to discuss medicine with people incapable of understanding:

"For the time being, thanks to the second injection, she's unconscious and she'll only come to in the nursing home."

Until then I had had the impression of three almost unreal figures set in the emptiness of the house, and the silence that seemed to emanate from the dead man gave the voices of my mother and Florian an unusual tonality.

A stifled bell ringing somewhere, in a nearby room or in a corridor, acted as a signal. Within less than fifteen minutes, a mass of people had broken the stagnation of the air and the rooms were filled with strangers as well as some members of the family whom we had not seen come in.

The first person to arrive was the police inspector, accompanied by his secretary or assistant. They both looked solemn and their noses were red with cold.

My cousin introduced himself:

"Doctor Jean Floriau."

"I know you by name, doctor."

The inspector looked at my mother, then at me, questioningly.

"My aunt . . . cousin, Blaise Huet . . ."

During the course of the conversation between my mother and Floriau I had glanced furtively several times at the corpse, and it would not have surprised me if my uncle had opened his eyes and participated unexpectedly in what they were saying.

"Is she his sister?" asked the inspector.

"His sister-in-law."

The inspector cleared his throat as if he were waiting for something to happen, and Floriau understood.

"You ought to go and see Colette for a moment, Aunt . . ."

She withdrew reluctantly, but she was somewhat reassured by the fact that I was allowed to remain and the last look she gave me before going out of the door contained a recommendation.

Looking for the first time at the bed in front of him, the inspector crossed himself and stood motionless for a moment as though he were observing a minute's silence at a meeting. He then pointed at the bottle on the bed table.

"I suppose they're sleeping pills? Were you his doctor?"

"I examined him on two or three occasions, I think, but he had a regular doctor, my colleague Bonnard."

"Was it he who prescribed these for him?"

"With my full consent. My uncle didn't take them regularly. Only when he couldn't sleep."

"Of course, he knew how many he could take?"

"He was a prudent man. According to François, the butler, the bottle was opened about a week ago, so there could only have been half a dozen tablets missing. Judging from what's left, my uncle must have swallowed about thirty last night."

"I hear his wife was out?"

"I took her to the Grand Théâtre, where there was a gala performance, and I dropped her at the front door at about twelve."

"You didn't come up?"

"No. When I arrived home she had already telephoned my wife to tell her what had happened and to ask me to come over immediately."

"About what time do you think your uncle died?"

There was a sound of heavy steps, voices, and bumps

on the staircase. François came into the room and spoke to my cousin in a whisper.

"Just a minute, inspector. The stretcher-bearers have come to take my aunt to the Saint Joseph Nursing Home . . ."

Some men in white coats, with white caps on their heads like surgeons, crossed the room, hesitated for an instant when they saw the dead man, probably wondering whether it was he they had to take away.

The inspector and his companion spoke to each other in an undertone and the assistant wrapped the medicine bottle in a handkerchief and put it into his overcoat pocket.

"The glass, too?" he asked.

"I don't think that will be necessary."

I looked around on hearing a strange little sob and I was surprised to see that it was my mother who was crying. The door of the adjoining room was open. A nurse in a gray-blue uniform was helping the stretcher-bearer lay the inert body of my aunt on the stretcher, and she wiped away a drop of saliva from her mouth.

I suppose poor François spent all his time going up and down the stairs, because I now met Monique, Floriau's wife, who had come to join her husband and was looking for him in the various rooms. No sooner did I lose sight of her than the men from the morgue bumped into my aunt's stretcher-bearers. The two groups of men knew each other and exchanged some mysterious signs of greeting.

"I wonder," my mother said in my ear, "if you shouldn't telephone your brother."

After Colette had gone we were asked to leave the room so that Uncle Antoine's body could be taken away. We went through a bathroom that we had never seen before and found ourselves in a boudoir draped in pearl-gray silk where a pair of cherry-colored satin slippers were still lying on the floor and a dressing gown had been thrown over the back of the chair.

"Antoine's leaving, too," sighed my mother.

Didn't that mean that, apart from old François and the sixteen-year-old maid, there would be nobody in the house?

I saw the inspector and his companion on the landing again, where Floriau was shaking hands with them. At the same time, I was surprised to see my brother coming up the stairs. What probably amazed me most of all was the pipe in his mouth, as though he had merely come to write a report for his newspaper.

Lucien is three years younger than I, but it seems to me that life has marked him more deeply. He's hard up, with a wife and three children to support. Not only does he work every night at *Le Nouvelliste* as a subeditor, but he also reports on local matters for some papers in Paris and writes several columns each week.

Untidy in his appearance, he affects a certain negligence and his teeth are as yellow as if he had never brushed them.

"How did you know?"

"When I telephoned the various police stations, as I do every morning, a sergeant whom I know told me that my uncle was dead . . . and that the inspector had been called.

Does Mother know?" At that very moment they carried the body past and we had to squeeze against the wall. On the stairway I heard a woman's voice asking:

"Who made that decision?"

I immediately recognized the voice of Aunt Juliette, my father's and Antoine's sister, the one who married Lemoine, the carrier, and, as soon as he had died, started to run his moving business.

She had to stop on the first floor to let the men from the morgue pass with their burden, and I again heard her resonant voice.

"So I'm not entitled to see him?"

My mother joined my brother and me on the landing, while Floriau and his wife whispered to each other in my uncle's room, by the empty bed.

"What's going on?"

Aunt Juliette appeared on the stairs, by no means out of breath, in her hand the umbrella she used as a walking stick because she had had trouble with her legs. I hadn't seen her for at least two years and it had then only been accidentally, when I ran into her in a department store.

"Who on earth made all these decisions? I can understand their sending Colette to a nursing home. They should have done that years ago! But that they should take away my brother's body without my even being able to see him on his deathbed . . ."

She looked at my mother.

"So you're here! With your two sons . . ."

My aunt had brought only one of her sons, the

youngest, Maurice, who helps her in the carrier business. I hadn't realized he was there. Like his mother, he had been held up by the procession coming down the stairs. After pausing to ask François some questions, he was the last to arrive on the landing.

"I'll tell you, Aunt . . ."

Floriau confronted her, both respectfully and firmly.

"I'm terribly sorry to appear to be butting in on something that doesn't concern me. However, despite appearances to the contrary, I have no say in the decisions that have been made . . . Uncle Antoine committed suicide and the law is very precise . . ."

"How do you know he committed suicide? Did he leave a letter?"

"We haven't found anything. The medical evidence allows no room for doubt."

"Was it you who gathered this evidence?"

He remained perfectly calm and his wife came up to him as if to provide him with her silent assistance.

"The coroner came first thing this morning. The police inspector left the house a moment ago . . ."

"So, on the pretext that he committed suicide, my poor brother is going to be carved up. . . ."

What made the scene even more grotesque was that it all took place on the landing, which was fortunately quite large, in front of the open door of the room where one could see the unmade bed and where nobody dared enter.

None of us, however many of us there were, had been a regular visitor of the house and consequently nobody took the initiative of invading one of the rooms—of going down to the dining room on the first floor, for instance, or of entering one of the dark drawing rooms on the ground floor.

"What did Colette say before she left? She's his wife, after all, whether one likes it or not."

"She didn't say anything. She has had a violent shock. She tried to kill herself last night . . ."

"Do you think she's mad?"

"It's not for me to say. I personally don't think she's mad, but she's certainly not in her normal state of mind at the moment."

"How long is this abnormal state going to last?"

"By now she's already in the hands of a specialist . . ."

My aunt Juliette is thickset, like a man, with a man's shoulders and a man's movements and an almost masculine voice. Her son, who was standing next to her, didn't breathe a word and one felt that he was accustomed to not speaking in his mother's presence. I looked at him attentively. It seemed to me that he, of all of us, was the most alien in this house. He is a big boy with heavy features and a plebeian look about him. He didn't know where to put his large hands and occasionally cast a furtive, almost frightened glance into the room.

It had always been thought in the family that Aunt Juliette had married beneath her when she wedded Lemoine, who had started off as a truck driver.

"Who's going to look after everything for the time being?"

It was again Aunt Juliette who spoke and who seemed to take the situation in hand.

"Look after what?" asked my mother with feigned ingenuousness.

"He'll have to be buried, won't he? Who's going to send out the notifications, organize the church service, and so on?"

To my amazement my brother broke in:

"The Church does not allow a religious service in the event of suicide . . ."

"And how does the Church know? Does it know what we aren't even sure of ourselves? That man died alone, in his bed, and what actually happened is nobody's business. . . ."

My brother has remained very devout. He's a militant Catholic, and for a long time he was head of the parish club.

"One can't cheat," he said.

"Who said anything about cheating? I know just as much about religion as you do. Nobody can tell what my brother was thinking about when he died. Nobody can even swear that he was in his right mind when he took those pills . . ."

We looked at each other awkwardly, because nobody had an answer to my aunt's question—who was going to see to the notifications, the announcements in the paper, the funeral?

I looked at my brother. I was sure that he was longing to volunteer, not out of self-interest or to prove his mettle or to play an important part, but simply because he is the man who always agrees to do what nobody else wants to do. In the various societies of which he is a member, especially the benevolent societies, one can be sure of seeing his name followed by the words "assistant secretary" or "assistant treasurer," which means that it is he who does all the work.

Yet, of all of us, Lucien is the one in the worst health. His wife is not healthy either. One of his children is always ill, but this doesn't stop him from doing the most exhausting chores at the end of the day, which nobody obliges him to do.

Basically, I almost envy him and I wonder whether, although he is the poorest, he is not the happiest of the Huets.

I noticed my mother nudging him. At first he turned toward her as if to protest, but then he murmured:

"If there's nobody else . . ."

Aunt Juliette didn't turn a hair.

"There must be an address book with a list of people to inform. And, mind you, don't forget Aunt Sophie. Break the news to her tactfully, if Monique hasn't already done so."

Monique shook her head.

"François will certainly find it for you . . . Where is François?"

The old manservant emerged from a room I had never been in.

"Perhaps you could serve us a drink, my poor François. What are we all doing here on the landing?"

She preceded us down the stairs, still holding her

umbrella, followed by her great lout of a son, and the others filed after her into the dining room, the door of which she opened authoritatively.

"Have you got any port?"

Her father, Jules Huet, who once owned the Hôtel and the Restaurant du Globe on Rue des Chartreux, went down in the family history as a man who liked to have a drink with his clients. They even say that he died the day after the armistice because he had caroused until dawn.

"If he hadn't drunk so much," my mother used to repeat to me, "he would have lived as long as his wife."

Was that why my father never touched any spirits and rarely even had a glass of wine? My uncle Fabien didn't drink, either. Antoine, who had just died by his own hand, simply had an *apéritif* before dinner.

It was apparently Juliette, the only girl in the family, who had inherited her father's taste and she reputedly drank gallons of red wine with her drivers.

As François placed some crystal glasses on the table and Aunt Juliette sank onto a chair, Floriau pulled his watch out of his pocket.

"I must go to the Saint Joseph Nursing Home," he said, looking around for his wife.

She understood.

"Can you drop me at home on the way?"

Two fewer of us. There were now five people seated in front of the seven glasses, Aunt Juliette, her son Maurice, my mother, my brother Lucien, and myself. François poured out the port with the unsteady hand of an old man.

There was a long silence. My mother decided to sit down, too. So did Maurice, while my brother and I remained standing. Through the two tall windows I could see the trees on the embankment, the gray water of the river being whipped into little white waves, people crossing the bridge carrying chrysanthemums.

My aunt sighed and reached out for her glass.

"Your health . . ."

And we repeated in turn, as though we were answering at Mass:

"Your health . . ."

"Your health . . ."

"*Your* health, Juliette," added my mother.

We clinked glasses out of habit. François had retired discreetly into the pantry. I don't know what had become of the little maid, whom I hadn't seen all morning. Maybe she had fallen asleep, fully dressed, on her bed?

A life-size portrait of my uncle dressed in a lawyer's gown with his insignia as Grand Officier de la Légion d'Honneur, dominated us silently and inertly.

"Well," said my aunt, after draining her glass, "I'll be curious to know about all the intrigues behind this business!"

She seemed to be looking for some support from us. But we remained silent, embarrassed. Even my mother, who was thinking the same thing but who preferred to leave the responsibility of the first offensive to a real Huet, said nothing.

"You must think it is strange," Juliette continued,

"that my brother should have done something like this the very evening Colette went out with that pretentious Floriau . . ."

She turned toward my brother, as though Lucien knew more about it than the rest of us.

"Is it true that they went out together frequently?"

And Lucien answered awkwardly:

"I believe so."

Then she picked on my mother:

"You know the Restaurant de la Huchette in the Bois de La Barraude? No! Of course, you never go outside your neighborhood. It appears that it's not only a restaurant frequented by high society, but also that it has rooms. One of my sons-in-law, Ernest, who's got a quarry not far from there, says that he's seen Floriau's car in front of the place on several occasions . . . and, at least once, he recognized Colette leaving with him . . ."

She looked at us again, one by one, as if to force us to take a stand.

"And that's the man who's now talking about suicide and an autopsy. . . . Would that have happened if he hadn't been sleeping with his aunt?"

She got up, relieved, poured herself out a glass, which she drained at a draught, and, turning toward her son, commanded:

"Come along, Maurice!"

When she reached the door, she turned around as though she were suddenly worried.

"Are you all staying here?"

My mother dashed over to her.

"No! I'm coming with you, Juliette . . ."

I remained alone with my brother in front of the seven glasses and Lucien murmured:

"I must ask François for the address book."

Without saying anything, I went with him.

The Same Day, Ten O'clock
at Night

I wrote the last pages in the course of the afternoon, because
two days a week, Tuesdays and Thursdays, I have classes
only in the morning. Thanks to my uncle Antoine, I got a
job as a drawing teacher at the Academy of Arts, whose
vast, cold rooms with huge, curtainless bay windows
overlooking courtyards and roofs, are part of the picture
gallery.

The Academy was built at the same time as the
Conservatoire and the Grand Théâtre, around the middle
of the last century, when the town was at the height of its
industrial prosperity.

In spite of generations after generations of students, the
school has not produced a single painter of any real value.
Some acquired local fame and one can find paintings by
some of the older students in houses like that of my uncle.
Others went to Paris, exhibited once or twice at the Salon
d'Automne, and finally sank into anonymity.

So this morning I taught about forty boys and girls,

mostly girls, between sixteen and eighteen years old, dressed in white coveralls. It is what is known in school jargon as a "plaster class." Throughout an entire year my students make charcoal drawings of plaster casts of classical statues, first a foot, then a hand, then a torso, and finally a head with the blind eyes of a Roman emperor.

This afternoon Irène went out to do some shopping, go to the hairdresser, and God knows what else, and I availed myself of the opportunity to write.

Nicolas Macherin came to dinner early and seemed to me to have put on weight. At the age of fifty-eight, he weighs close to two hundred pounds and has started to walk with his paunch jutting out and his legs spread slightly apart.

His doctor begs him to go on a diet and constantly prods him to take some exercise, but he pays no more attention to his figure than he seems to pay to his health. It is as though he enjoys being fat, to the point of grotesqueness. He eats three times as much as I do. That's his great pleasure in life.

When he dines with us, which he does at least three times a week, and sometimes four or even five times, he calls my wife in advance to discuss the menu with her.

Particularly during the game season (which is on just at the moment), he likes to go to the market on his way to the office and have some partridges, woodcock, or a haunch of venison or boar sent to us.

He also decides about the wine and it is he who has furnished our cellar.

He is reputed to be a hard, ruthless businessman. His colleagues, his office staff, and his workmen are terrified of him. I think this is because his big face can turn stony from one moment to the next. That never happens when he's with us. At our house he becomes a jovial, good-natured man who takes a surprising pleasure in hearing naïve or vulgar stories.

But I can remember several occasions when we had guests (chosen by him, incidentally, since he has a horror of intruders). If one of them was deceived by his good humor and tried to extract some financial information from him or obtain some personal advantage, the iron curtain would come down; he would assume a fixed expression, his face turning lifeless, without a trace of human warmth, and the importunate individual would feel he had become an object.

I know people think that even if I keep up appearances in public, I toe the line when I'm at home and pay for the comfort and luxury that surround me with continual humiliations.

They would be very surprised to see the three of us at table or taking coffee and a liqueur in the living room after the meal. Whether they believe it or not, there is absolutely no sense of embarrassment between us.

This evening, maybe because it was exactly a week after my uncle Antoine's death, we found ourselves discussing him. Nicolas Macherin knew him well. They had belonged to the same set and had met in places to which I could never go and about which I only have a vague idea.

"I turned to him for advice on several occasions," said Nicolas. "He once saved me several millions. His death will leave a gap, because I don't know of anyone fit to replace him."

If my uncle, who had never appeared in the assize court, was little known by the general public, he was extremely well known in a certain range of society, the range of big business, both on a national and an international level. He was an expert in international law and it had several times been suggested that he join the Court of The Hague.

He was less a lawyer than a jurist, and the cases he looked after rarely reached the civil courts. Two or three times a month he took a plane to Basel, Milan, London or Amsterdam, not to mention Paris, where he always had the same suite in a discreet hotel on the Left Bank.

The family knew nothing about that aspect of Antoine's life, and yet we regarded him as our great man. It was to him that we turned, diffidently, in moments of difficulty.

He received us cordially. It never occurred to him to disown any of us, not even Edouard, toward whom he displayed a far greater leniency than did the rest of the family.

He attended all the Huet marriages, and, at the banquets, he was somewhat isolated by our embarrassment and our respect.

I now wonder if it was not he who was embarrassed about not being on the same level as the rest of the family.

I'm sure it gave him pleasure when he saw one of us come into his study. His little eyes lighted up whenever he came into contact with us, as though he had recovered something of his childhood.

"How are you, son? And how's Irène?"

He never forgot a name, never confused the various branches of the family. My brother, Lucien, for example, had been surprised to hear him ask for news of his youngest child, whom our uncle had never seen and whose birth he had only been informed of by a printed announcement.

"Tell me, son."

He called us all son. He knew that if we went to see him it was not a casual visit made on our way past the imposing building on Quai Notre Dame.

When I had just got married and was hard up, I told him about the job as a drawing teacher which was open at the Academy of Arts. He simply asked me:

"Who's the person who controls the job?"

"I suppose it's the director."

He shook his head.

"No. The director's a subordinate. I assume that the Academy is administered by the city."

"I think so."

"In that case, it's the mayor's decision. He's a radical socialist. I know the leader of his party."

He picked up the receiver. As you see, it all took place way above the head of an obscure would-be art teacher.

Uncle Antoine lived in a completely different world from ours. He inhabited a universe where all our notions

must have seemed ridiculous and petty. When Uncle
Fabien died and there was some trouble about Aunt
Sophie's right to a pension owing to some administrative
hairsplitting, he applied to the minister in person and the
whole business was settled within three days.

"Do you think he committed suicide, Nic?" asked my
wife.

"I suppose he must have, since everybody seems to
agree about it."

"Because of his wife?"

"It's possible. But that's not necessarily the reason."

"What other reason could he have had for killing
himself? His doctor says that he didn't have cancer or any
other incurable disease. He wasn't ill. I shouldn't think he
had any financial problems."

Nicolas turned slowly toward Irène, smiling rather
tenderly, a smile a little like the one I thought I saw on my
uncle's lips the morning of Allhallows. I think this annoyed
my wife.

"Why do you look at me as though I were a silly girl
talking rubbish?"

"Not at all. You're delightful, Irène, but you can't
understand."

"What is there to understand? One doesn't kill oneself
for no reason, does one?"

"There are many reasons for dying."

"Which, for instance?"

He made a vague gesture with his chubby hand and

went on eating. As usual, Irène had to go on. She never drops a subject unless she thinks she's won.

"Did he really love her?"

"He loved her in his own way."

"What does that mean?"

"He wanted to make her happy. He needed to make somebody happy, at least one person."

"Why did he choose her, a completely unbalanced girl? She sometimes used to spend three or four days in bed, her curtain drawn, without even letting him into her room, and then again she would get frantically restless. She was mad, wasn't she?"

Still with the shade of an indulgent smile, as though he was unaware that my wife loathes tolerance more than anything else, Nicolas replied, peeling his pear:

"I don't know."

"You dined with them frequently. You saw them together. Apparently, Colette might get up in front of ten or twelve guests and go to her room without saying a word and stay there for the rest of the evening. Is that true?"

"I saw her do it once."

"What did he say?"

"He turned pale, not from anger, as one might think, but from anxiety. He thought up a more or less plausible excuse for his guests and, when the meal was over, he went upstairs to ask her how she was through the door."

"So she didn't give a damn about him?"

"I don't think that's true."

"But she slept with other men all the same. Isn't it true that once she had been away for three or four days and was found ill, in a dirty hotel room where she had gone with a stranger? They even say that after two nights the stranger left her, taking her bag, her jewels, and her fur coat."

"I heard about that."

"Is it true or not?"

"It's perfectly plausible."

"And you think this woman loved him?"

For Irène, such an affirmation was an insult. She was humiliated by it and I could see that she was on the verge of tears. Nicolas noticed that, too, and tried to settle everything by some vague generalizations, without actually taking back what he had said.

"There are many kinds of love . . ."

"Would you like that sort of love?"

It was a challenge. They were about to have a scene, but they both had to go to the theater where a company on tour was performing one of the latest hits from Paris.

"I wouldn't personally. There were some very considerable differences between your uncle and me."

She couldn't help hissing:

"I should hope so!"

Nicolas and I had avoided catching each other's eye in order not to make matters worse with the smile that we would inevitably have exchanged.

My wife went to make up her face again and get her mink. Contrary to what one might have expected, Macherin and I did not comment on the incident once we were alone. We never talk about Irène with each other or about anything to do with her.

We simply made some trite remarks about the play they were going to see and the chances of snow, for, although the storm has ceased and it is no longer raining, the sky has turned an ominous white. It is very low, very heavy, and this afternoon, shortly before dusk, there was a vibration in the air, barely visible and icy dust that could easily turn into snowflakes.

I said quite naturally:

"Have a good time."

After the theater Irène will certainly suggest drinking a bottle of champagne at the Tabarin, a new nightclub where they have a fairly good floor show that goes on until two in the morning. So I'm sure of not being disturbed in my study. The decorator who arranged the apartment fixed up, at my request, a small study for me, which is both modern and comfortable, next to the living room. Maybe because of Uncle Antoine, I insisted on having a fireplace and, from time to time, I get up in order to put on another log.

This evening I would like to finish my account of Allhallows because other things have happened since and I might get them mixed up.

I looked at my watch when François went upstairs once again after showing out Aunt Juliette, my cousin, and my mother. My brother and I had left the dining room, where there was nothing else to do, and we waited for him in the hall on the first floor, at the head of the double staircase with its red carpet, which he climbed slowly, his head bent forward, so that all we could see was his bald pate. He seemed to be talking to himself under his breath and for some reason he reminded me of a sacristan. He has the same colorless complexion, the silent gait, the unctuous gestures.

I thought that the address book we were waiting for must be in my uncle's study or in the long library next to it, which, because of its wood paneling and what I had just thought about François, appeared to me like a sacristy. It excited me to enter those rooms again, rooms that had always impressed me, now that my uncle was dead.

Sometimes, when I have nothing to do, I go to auction sales simply in order to see inside people's lives, especially if they are people I used to know, to get an idea of the setting in which they lived and the objects that surrounded them.

One day, on the sidewalk, they sold the furniture of an old magistrate who lived on the street where I was born, two steps from our house.

When we were children, we used to poke fun at that austere, grumpy old fellow who called the police every time we rang his bell or our rubber ball broke one of his windows. He was a widower and lived with an old maid. What was my surprise to discover that he slept in a large Louis XV bed, had a drawing room covered in buttercup silk, and collected eighteenth-century erotic engravings.

I had never really looked at my uncle's study because I had only been in there in his presence and he intimidated me. I had fragmentary memories of it, a vague and general impression.

"Listen, François . . ."

My brother was talking. He was still in his overcoat, as was I, because that morning nobody except Floriau had dared put himself at ease.

"Yes, Monsieur Lucien?"

François knew the family just as well as my uncle did. He had seen us when we were children. It was with him that we sought refuge when our parents had visited my uncle in his study.

"In order to send out the notifications I need a list of people who used to see my uncle. I assume he had an address book?"

I think that Lucien was as nonplused as I was when the butler replied:

"There must be several, but I wouldn't know where they were. I wasn't allowed to touch any book or any paper. It's Mademoiselle Jeanne who knows about all that."

In the bustle of that morning none of us had thought about my uncle's secretary. Admittedly, I would not even have recognized her in the street. I only remembered a rather fat woman whom I saw in the library when I came to call on my uncle, and she may have appeared briefly a couple of times in his study.

"I suppose she won't be coming today?"

"It's Allhallows, sir."

"And tomorrow is All Souls' Day. She'll probably have that off, too."

"Probably."

"Have you got her address?"

"I have her telephone number in the pantry. Do you want to try to call her?"

François did not invite us into the study. I was sure he did it on purpose, that he regarded the place as sacred. He had had to open up the rooms on the second floor, and then the dining room, on Aunt Juliette's order. Now that the house was calmer, he had again become the guardian of the treasures, the priest officiating at a sort of cult.

The secretary's address and telephone number were on a list hanging above the telephone in the pantry, where we had followed the butler.

"Would you like to call her?"

My brother dialed the number and waited for some time.

"Mademoiselle Chambovet?"

The voice at the other end of the line was so loud that I heard every word.

"No. This is her mother."

"Could I talk to your daughter?"

"She won't be back before half past twelve or one. She's gone to the cemetery. Who's speaking?"

"I'm calling from Quai Notre Dame."

"Is that Monsieur Huet?"

The voice had become respectful.

"No. His nephew. My uncle has had an accident and I need to see your daughter as soon as possible. I live in the same part of town as you. If you don't mind, I'll come around shortly."

"You don't mean to say that he's dead?"

"Yes."

"Did he have a heart attack?"

"He's dead. I'll be around at once."

François made no attempt to hold us back. I wondered whether he would have the strength to cook himself lunch. There was still no sign of the little maid, who must have been asleep. Wouldn't François, who hadn't been to bed all night, have a rest, too? I thought of the house, empty except for those two beings asleep in their rooms on the third floor, under the roof, and all the other floors dead, left to themselves.

He followed us toward the staircase and I needed a certain amount of courage to turn toward him.

"Tell me, François, you who knew him well . . ."

"Yes, Monsieur Blaise?"

"Did they ever quarrel? Recently, I mean . . ."

"Never, sir."

He said that with an almost offended expression, as though I had just uttered a blasphemy.

"How about her?"

"You know what Madame is like. She has her good days and her bad days. It's not her fault."

"Was she disagreeable to him?"

"There were times when she didn't want to see anybody. She sometimes spent as much as two days in her room without eating. Then Monsieur Huet would tell me, anywhere up to two or twenty times a day, 'Go and listen, François.'

"He was worried, unhappy. He didn't dare go up himself for fear of upsetting her still more. When I came down he used to ask me, 'Is she crying?'

"Sometimes she used to cry her eyes out, with sobs that one could hear on the landing. Other times she simply groaned gently, like an animal.

"When I told Monsieur Huet that I didn't hear anything he would be still more worried.

" 'Did you try to open the door?'

" 'Yes, sir. It's locked.'

" 'Did you look through the keyhole?'

" 'Yes, sir. Madame looks as though she's asleep.'

"He sometimes even interrupted an important conference with gentlemen who had come from abroad to see him."

"Was he afraid that she would kill herself?"

François nodded.

"Did she ever talk about it?"

"No, but she tried twice. The first time was in the house she lived in before they were married, and the second was four years ago."

"Was my uncle angry about her going to the concert with Floriau?"

"On the contrary. It was he who got Mademoiselle Jeanne to reserve seats. You know how he was. He hated going out at night. He realized that Madame needed distractions and it was always he who invited the doctor to dinner."

"Wasn't he jealous?"

François lowered his eyes modestly and replied:

"I don't know, Monsieur Blaise."

François has been married, over forty years ago, to one of my uncle's maids, who died giving birth, together with her child, and I wonder if he has so much as touched a woman since.

"Did he say anything to you yesterday that would account for . . ."

"No, sir."

"Did you serve dinner?"

"Yes, sir. They dined early with Monsieur Floriau because of the concert."

"How was my uncle?"

"As usual. They spoke about music all through the meal."

"Did my uncle know much about music?"

"There are hundreds of records up there and he often used to play them as he worked at night."

"Was my aunt in a good mood?"

"She was wearing a new saffron-yellow dress and she looked pleased when Monsieur Floriau complimented her about it."

"You mustn't mind my asking these questions, François, I'm trying to understand . . ."

"Everybody's trying to understand, Monsieur Blaise."

I may be wrong, but I shuddered at the time because it

seemed to me that the butler gave a mysterious meaning to his words. Was he alluding to his own situation? I don't think so. But all the same his words shook me and, as I crossed beneath the archway, I felt a chill down my spine.

"Have you got your car?" asked Lucien once we were on the sidewalk, where the wind lashed against us.

"No, I came on foot with Mother."

Lucien doesn't have a car. During the week when on an urgent job, he takes one of the old cars or motorbikes belonging to the newspaper. Otherwise he goes by streetcar.

I said, turning up my coat collar:

"I'll go some of the way with you . . . ."

We hadn't walked together in the street for a long time. It brought back the time when, as a young man, I used to walk up and down the Rue de la Cathédrale and the Rue des Chartreux for hours with a couple of friends, especially Denèvre.

I've been only briefly in Paris and in one or two other big cities. I've never really lived in one. I think that the most typical and agonizing aspect of life in a large provincial town, especially for a young man, are those endless, pointless walks along the same streets, with the same window displays year after year and the same familiar faces.

Ernest Denèvre was my fellow student at the school of architecture, but, unlike me, he finished his studies. He and I could never make up our minds to go home. He lived at the other end of town, up on the hill, not far from where my brother lives now, and we used to come out of the café, our café, the Moderne—each group has its own special café and never goes to any other; on Rue de la Cathédrale there are five cafés in a row.

We walked back and forth, looking into the cafés, where people seemed to be fixed in front of the tables and the hands of the clock seemed to move more slowly than anywhere else.

"I'll come along some of the way . . ."

I wonder now what we can have talked about like that, every day, for hours on end. We would get to Avenue de la Gare, where Denèvre was supposed to catch his streetcar, and this time it would be he who suggested:

"I'll go as far as the bridge with you . . ."

And so, before we separated in the ever more empty streets where we ended up hearing only our own footsteps, we would reaccompany each other two or three times.

On Allhallows I had no desire to go home straightaway. Nicolas Macherin was supposed to lunch with us and we weren't going to eat before one o'clock or perhaps even half past one. For no apparent reason, my wife, who never goes to Mass, takes longer to get ready on Sunday than on any other day.

I also think that, because of Antoine's death and the family reunion that morning, I suddenly felt closer to Lucien. I may even have felt a certain tenderness toward him.

Of all the people who had been at the house on Quai Notre Dame that morning, of all the people we had spoken about, he was the humblest, the poorest, and also the most

eager to help. Of all the Huets, he is the only one whom I
have never heard complain and the first words he said to
me on the embankment, shoving his hands into his pockets,
were typical of him:

"Fortunately, there's now a Mass at five in the
afternoon."

He had agreed to see to all the formalities entailed by
my uncle's death and he was thinking about his Mass.

"I'll have to pass by the diocese," he added. "I hope I
can persuade them to provide a funeral service after all."

"Uncle Antoine didn't practice. He probably didn't
even believe."

"He went to services as long as his mother was alive,"
Lucien replied calmly.

"That doesn't mean anything."

"It can mean a great deal. I know that he also took on
several ecclesiastical lawsuits free of charge."

"Why do you think he committed suicide?"

"I don't even try to understand."

"Do you think it's because of Colette and Floriau? You
heard what Aunt Juliette said about their meetings at La
Huchette?"

"I knew about that," answered my brother.

We arrived on Rue de la Cathédrale, which lacked the
customary animation of Sundays and holidays, not only
because of the weather but because most people were at the
cemetery. It was so dark that the lights were on in the cafés
and the faces seemed deformed by the mist on the windows.

"Don't you want a drink?"

"You know I can't really, not with my stomach . . ."

In addition to everything else, Lucien suffered from indigestion.

"I wonder," I went on, "whether Floriau is really in love."

"Probably. Our cousin Monique is a good girl. She's been well brought up. She's an excellent housewife and an exceptionally good mother. No matter what time of the day it is, she always looks neat and fresh."

"So does he."

"Yes, but he's more complicated than she is. He has other problems, other interests in life. Colette is a musician. She's studied painting. She's read everything."

He was about to add something else, but he faltered and it was I who went on:

"And, above all, she's attractive."

That's true. My aunt Colette, at the age of forty, is undoubtedly the most attractive, the most exciting woman in town. I don't know why that is, but the fact remains that all men turn around to stare at her when she walks down the street and, for a few seconds at least, they all want to go to bed with her.

She always looks as though she were eager to confide in you, to establish an immediate link with you.

Her body is supple, on the verge of plumpness, and when one sees her move in the street one can't help imagining her in the bedroom. Even her black, rebellious hair, with a lock that constantly falls onto her full cheeks, is the most sensual hair I know.

I have desired her, too. Everybody has desired her. And what my mother calls her madness, her instability, her sudden fears, her way of withdrawing into herself like an animal sensing danger, makes her still more attractive.

One feels that one wants to protect her from the world, from others, from herself. She's the sort of woman whom one would like to place with care, like a precious object, in the luxurious seclusion of a harem.

Had honest Lucien felt that, too? Had he felt the same urge of desire? If so, I'm sure that he immediately felt ashamed and had gone to confession.

"Now she's free. I shouldn't think they'll keep her in a nursing home forever."

Lucien could guess what I was thinking. What would become of her if she were left to herself? Had Uncle Antoine kept the vow he made to his mother? Had he left his fortune and the house on Quai Notre Dame to Colette, or had he simply assured an income for her?

Would Floriau be tempted to play his part as protector to the very end, and in that case what would happen to his marriage?

I, for one, was sure that Uncle Antoine had made a deliberate choice of our cousin in order to keep his wife away from the disastrous sort of affair that Irène had so ferociously mentioned at dinner.

But it was about three years ago that Floriau had become a regular visitor to the house. Had my uncle foreseen, ever since then, that he would prefer to back out one day?

Was he not a man who saw much further than we did, a man with an almost terrifying lucidity?

It was Allhallows, I remember, a week ago tomorrow, when I walked along with my brother and thought these things. Nicolas had not yet spoken to me about my uncle as he did that evening. I tried, from scattered fragments, from what various people had said, to get some idea of what was happening.

I admit that I was quite excited by what had taken place and by everything that I foresaw. One day, as I said at the beginning, I wrote my story, our story, the story of myself, my wife, and Nicolas, and I was made to feel ashamed of it, either deliberately or otherwise.

This time it was not only my circumscribed world that had come into play, but the entire family circle. For years we had each lived in our own part of town, each within our own means, habits, problems, personal pleasures, having only occasional contact with one another.

But now all the Huets, including Aunt Juliette, whom I hardly ever heard about and whose children I barely knew—now all the Huets, I repeat, were meeting face to face. They were again revealing themselves and were probably about to confront one another.

That aroused a feeling of slight exultation as well as a subtle joy within me. I would like to have run from one to the other, to observe their reactions, to ask indiscreet questions.

I knew that they despised me, all of them except perhaps Lucien, who was too good a Christian to despise anyone and who simply pitied me and prayed for me.

But Lucien, too, was probably about to find himself in an awkward situation. Not knowing whether he had heard the news, I didn't dare mention it to him, and it was he himself who broached the subject as we stood waiting for the streetcar.

"Have you heard that Edouard is in town?" he asked me, almost incidentally.

"Mother mentioned it."

"He's been here for some days."

"Have you seen him?"

"No."

"Has he seen his wife?"

The red and yellow streetcar drew up ringing its bell, all lighted up like the cafés, with heads nodding at every jolt. My brother said to me very quickly, before jumping onto the platform:

"He's been living with her for two days."

I remained on the sidewalk watching Lucien smoking his pipe on the platform and preparing his change.

At one point, as my brother and I were going past Rue des Chartreux, it occurred to me to invite him to lunch at the restaurant, first of all for the pleasure of being alone with him, something that happens so rarely, and then because I had no desire to go home and to tell Irène and Nicolas about all that had happened since the morning.

I found myself unexpectedly plunged into the family, my family, which my wife had never really joined. Memories flowed back to me that accentuated the atmosphere of Allhallows.

I didn't know then that I would be recounting all the events that I was experiencing, so that I lived through them in all innocence, so to speak, without any care for logic. Thus, finding myself on the Rue des Chartreux after having accompanied Lucien to the streetcar, I suddenly went into the Hôtel du Globe, where, once I had entered the restaurant, I was enveloped in pungent warmth. It used to belong to my grandfather.

Although it has changed hands a couple of times since his death, it has hardly altered and remains just as bourgeois and just as welcoming.

Because it was Allhallows there weren't many people seated at the tables. The waiters and the cashier don't know me, and I sat in a corner near a window.

Maybe because I haven't traveled very much the Globe remains a unique place as far as I am concerned, with old-fashioned charm and a pleasant atmosphere. Although there are four or five more modern and more comfortable hotels in town, one of which was built quite recently, and also some more famous or more picturesque restaurants, the Globe has kept, year after year, its unchanged clientele of serious and prosperous businessmen from nearby towns, industrialists, landowners, and merchants. During the week it's almost impossible to find a table, and almost everybody knows everybody else—they greet each other and get up to shake hands.

There are no exposed beams across the ceiling, no red-checked tablecloths, no copper utensils hanging from the walls. It is like being in an old provincial house, the house of a notary, for instance, light and tidy.

After ordering oysters and a steak, I made for the telephone.

"Irène? It's me . . . Yes, everything went off all right . . . or, rather, as well as possible."

Her voice on the telephone surprises me every time; it seems somebody else's voice, sharper and drier than usual.

"Has Nicolas arrived? . . . You're expecting him at

any moment? . . . I'm calling to say that I won't be home for lunch . . . No, I'm no longer with my mother . . . I've just left Lucien . . . I'm in town, yes, and I've still got a number of things to do. . . ."

She didn't insist, and simply told me that Nic had just called her and was going to take her to Parantray after lunch.

"Have a good time . . . All right . . . if you're not back in time for dinner, I'll start eating. Besides, I don't even know if I'll be in myself."

Parantray was Macherin's castle, thirty miles out of town near Jugny, where the local rich go shooting. Nicolas doesn't shoot. All the same, almost every Sunday, he takes Irène down there in his black, chauffeur-driven Rolls. Sometimes I go with them, pick a gun from the rack in the hall, and go for a walk in the woods without bothering about the game. I don't like shooting, either. Besides, the country makes me sad, to the point of anguish.

I went back into the dining room and started thinking about Lucien, about the invitation I almost made and how it would probably have astonished him.

Indeed, my brother isn't the sort of man who goes to restaurants, except when he's traveling. They remain a luxury for him that he has to offer his family once or twice a year.

We were both brought up in that spirit. We weren't poor. My father earned a reasonable living, but there were, nevertheless, some expenses which seemed unnecessary, habits that belonged to a different set than ours.

Lucien had remained on the same social level. He may even have gone down a few pegs.

As I ate my oysters I tried to imagine my grandfather, Jules Huet, small, squat, like Uncle Antoine, in this house, which he had virtually created, and which he had made famous and prosperous.

The present proprietor, whom I knew by sight, no longer came to greet his clients; nor, once their meal was over, did he join them for a liqueur.

The cashier didn't look like my grandmother, either. I only knew her when she was an old woman. In our family album, which my mother keeps jealously, there is a portrait of her in her youth, with jutting breasts, fine features, and sparkling eyes.

I don't know of any photograph of my grandfather as a young man. Perhaps we will find some in Uncle Antoine's papers. He, the eldest, was the only one to know the full story of his parents. My father and Uncle Fabien talked relatively little about their father. As for Aunt Juliette, the youngest, she must know still less than the others. Besides, she is no longer really a Huet. She became a Lemoine and remained one after her husband's death.

For my part, I only know the broad outlines. My grandfather was the son of poor peasants. He was born on the Plateau de Berolles, the most arid part of the country, about twelve miles out of town. He had brothers and sisters, but I never heard anything about them. Every time I go through the village I look at the metal sign-board outside the inn, with the name of one Félicien Huet.

When he was quite young, my grandfather worked as a waiter in one of the cafés near the market where butchers and market gardeners used to have a snack at dawn. Some of those restaurants still exist, but I don't know which one he worked in.

He left for Paris at the time of the world exposition and worked in one of its restaurants; they say in the family that, by spending hardly anything and giving up smoking in order to economize, he came back with a lot of money.

Where did he meet my grandmother, Antoinette Aupic, of peasant stock herself, but from a more educated family?

I am now surprised about the scarcity of information we have about our ancestry and I regret not having asked Uncle Antoine about it; I am sure that he was the depositary of these secrets.

He was born in 1888, when his father was twenty-four and his mother twenty-one. So he shared their life before they settled at the Hôtel du Globe.

How had my grandfather been able to buy the hotel when he was still so young? Did he start off simply as a manager? Did a local bank lend him the sum he needed?

My father, too, was born elsewhere, on Rue du Clou, on the second floor of an old house, but his parents left it when he was five, so that all his memories were of the hotel on Rue des Chartreux. Like his brothers, Antoine and Fabien, he retained until the end a great tenderness, not to say veneration, for his mother, whom he went to see at least three times a week.

Nobody in the family was ever specific about it, but I have every reason to believe that, of Jules Huet and his wife, it was she who was the most enterprising, the most reliable, and the most intelligent.

Once his business had got going, I think that my grandfather started taking it easy, while my grandmother looked after everything—the linen, the staff, the kitchen.

How did she find time to look after her four children and make them do their homework? How, in the continuous bustle of a hotel, did she manage to preserve family life? And yet she did it, and that accounts for Uncle Antoine's passionate admiration for his mother.

Another point remains slightly obscure, too. Why and how, at my grandfather's death, was the family almost ruined? At the time, Antoine was thirty and was serving an apprenticeship with a lawyer who was also a senator. My father, who was younger, had just spent the four war years on the front and then in the hospital, because he had been gassed. Neither he nor his brother Fabien, who had come back from Germany where he had been a prisoner, were proposing to go into the hotel business.

Until then, business seems to have flourished. The hotel and the restaurant were always full. But there was no capital in the bank; new creditors appeared every day and the family had to sell.

Of the four children only the eldest, Antoine, had a job. He alone had been able to finish his expensive studies while the going was good. He alone, of all the sons, had

escaped military service, for reasons that I don't know
about.

If he really promised his mother that he would leave
his fortune to the Huets, this may well be why. It was as
though he had had more advantages than the others and
consequently owed compensation to them and to their
children. That would also explain why, in spite of his
position, he always received us with patient benevolence.

When Fabian was without a job and without any
special skills, it was Antoine who got him a job at the
municipal waterworks, where, thanks to his brother's protection, he soon became head manager. He also helped my
father set himself up as an architect. And finally, as I said, it
was through him that I obtained my job as a drawing
teacher.

Curiously enough, that hour I spent on my own, in my
corner, was one of the fullest of my life. It seems to me that I
sensed things which I am unable to express, subtle ties
between men, generations, and different destinies.

I, who usually drink very little, had a glass of port on
Quai Notre Dame and I ordered another as I was waiting
for the oysters. Then, together with the entrecôte à la
bordelaise, I was served a half-bottle of a fiery Burgundy
and, my eyelids smarting, I looked at the faces around me
as if I were dreaming. When the wine waiter suggested I
have an armagnac, I was unable to say no and I was given
it in a large brandy glass.

I had the impression that, although I remained myself,

I was leading several lives at the same time, that I was assuming various personalities which all suddenly seemed familiar to me. I even ordered a cigar, something I do very rarely, simply because I saw an old habitué lighting one with a beatific expression and that it reminded me of Uncle Antoine's cigars.

I must have been smiling happily as I enveloped myself in smoke and occasionally plunged my nose into my enormous snifter.

I was everywhere at the same time. I felt I could see my wife and Nicolas at home, alone together, my wife slightly suspicious, ready to take offense because she always thinks that people are making fun of her or that they think she can't understand. Both of them have an odd way of quarreling. He doesn't bat an eyelash. He just watches her work herself up, stamp her foot, and only his eyes sparkle, while his mouth assumes a distressed expression.

My mother was supposed to lunch alone in her apartment, awaiting the moment when she could recount the morning's events to her neighbors.

She was born above a hardware store on the narrow Rue du Petit-Vert, in the Saint-Eloi district, which is one of the most populous parts of the town. In marrying her, my father transplanted her into the Sainte-Barbe district, which was quieter and more bourgeois with its new houses.

No sooner was he dead and my brother and I had left her than she returned to her roots and settled two doors away from Rue du Petit-Vert, renewing her ties with people she hadn't seen for twenty years.

Nevertheless, she still keeps what I call the register of the Huets; she continues to see them from time to time, to take an interest in what they say and do. As a matter of fact, because of Nicolas and my wife, I'm the one she takes least interest in. I wonder what would happen if she suddenly found herself face to face with Irène.

I also thought of Uncle Fabien as I sipped my armagnac, of myself when I was sixteen, then twenty, then twenty-four, of myself on days like this, pacing the streets on my own, passing the closed shops, and occasionally, out of boredom, stopping in front of a shopwindow.

For a long time I had no friends, for, not knowing what I was going to do, I didn't find any group of which to be part. I'm going to write something paradoxical, a sentence that came to my mind that day, in the Restaurant du Globe, and which, maybe because of my state of semidrunkenness, seemed to me to be profound: *I was too ambitious to be part of a group!*

It seems less clear right now, but that was what I thought. This town, these streets where I walked for hours on end, these faces that are always the same, these names on the shopwindows filled me with something more than an almost painful sense of boredom; they filled me with a desire to escape, to escape anywhere, to flee in that unreasoning way in which one feels one is being pursued in a dream.

Well, also as in a dream, my feet were glued to the ground and I felt incapable of a forward movement.

I can say that I spent my adolescence, above all my

Sundays, flaunting my boredom and disgust with a sort of sensual pleasure.

I wanted to get away from this provincial life in which I felt bogged down. I would like to have had a prominent position, to have climbed very high, still higher than Uncle Antoine, whom I then regarded as a pitiful bourgeois.

How? By which career? I had no idea. I had been a mediocre student. I had no particular talent. Basically, I was already certain that I would never escape from myself, that at the age of thirty, fifty, or sixty I would still be walking along the same streets, stopping in front of the same shops, seeing the same windows illuminated with a syrupy light every evening.

So what was the point? What could I do, since nothing would get me anywhere?

One day, when I was seventeen and had just failed my second exams for the high-school certificate, I told my father that I wanted to go to art school and become a painter. It wasn't a vocation. The idea had occurred to me the day before when I passed a group of art students on Rue des Chartreux.

My father didn't flinch. He never flinched. He resigned himself. He already knew that he was ill. His doctor, we found out later, had told him quite frankly that he had only a few years left to live.

"Go to art school if you like. But since you must have some profession, I insist that you study architecture."

I studied architecture for only two years, because I had

no head for mathematics, which was why I'd failed my earlier exams.

That was where I met Denèvre, and from then on it was with him that I walked the streets of the town and sat for hours on end in the Café Moderne. Denèvre went on studying architecture. He was ugly, uglier than Uncle Antoine, obese and with a yellowish complexion. He had bad breath and never said anything that was not bitter and sarcastic.

I felt myself to be a failure. I got used to the idea and almost admired my own lucidity, drawing from it a secret pleasure.

Denèvre, on the other hand, swore to avenge himself. What for? For everything, and that undoubtedly included life.

He is now in Brazil, where he built some of the most modern buildings that one sees in magazines. Does he still remember our monotonous walks on Rue de la Cathédrale and Rue des Chartreux? Does he still remember me, who stayed behind?

In the manuscript that was returned to me so scornfully and that I now regret having destroyed, I wrote more extensively about this period of my life, which was essential for understanding the rest of the story. The novelist I sent it to thought that I was pitying myself, but I can say that he is wrong. I am mediocre, I know, but I am lucid and, I can add without excessive exaggeration, I am contented.

When I left the Globe, I returned to the north wind, the cold, the figures bent over and hugging the walls. I, too, leaned forward, my hands deep in my pockets, my nose frozen, and I crossed the Botanical Garden. I was in a state of euphoria and I found myself dragging my feet in the dead leaves as I had when I was a child.

"Pick up your feet, Blaise," my mother used to say to me.

A certain number of windows were lighted on Boulevard Joffre because the sky was getting darker and darker. I would like to have known what everybody was doing at home on a day like that. I've always been fascinated by windows, especially at night, when there are only a few lights on in a deserted street.

I must have rung the bell at the apartment; I hadn't taken my keys and Adèle, the maid, opened the door, a damp plate and a dishcloth in her hand.

"Has my wife left?"

"About twenty minutes ago."

"Anything happened?"

"There's just been a telephone call for you. Monsieur Lucien. He wants you to call him back as soon as you get in."

"At home?"

"He didn't say."

I took off my gloves, my coat, my hat, and left them in the hall. As I went through the dining room I caught a whiff of my wife's scent. I called my brother from the living room.

"I'm glad you're back. I was told you were lunching in town but nobody knew where and I wanted to tell you what was going on."

I didn't tell him I had lunched on my own at the Globe.

"Is there any news?"

"I've seen the secretary, Mademoiselle Jeanne, who is very cool and collected and knows what she's about. It's just as well that François put us in touch with her."

"Why?"

"Because we might have set about things the wrong way."

" 'Have you told the notary?' she asked me after the first emotional impact. 'Not yet? Have the seals been affixed?'

"None of us had thought about that. Yet an important inheritance is at stake. Nobody, except perhaps the notary, knows just what's in the will. Do you see?"

"I see!" I said.

It suddenly started to amuse me. All morning we had roamed about the house as though it belonged to us, admittedly under the surveillance of François. Hadn't he been the first person to be suspicious and to prevent us from getting the address book in my uncle's study? He prudently put us in touch with the secretary. Mademoiselle Jeanne, in her turn, told us to get in touch with the notary.

"His office can't be open today?" I said to my brother.

"Of course not. But Mademoiselle Jeanne gave me the

number of his home at Corbessière and I spoke to him on the telephone. He's called Gauterat . . ."

"I've seen his offices on Quai Colbert."

"Yes. He let me talk. He seems to be a cold, methodical man. When I asked him whether it was necessary to affix the seals he answered dryly:

" 'Absolutely! As long as the will hasn't been read the property has to be protected. I can't understand why the police inspector didn't raise the point . . .' "

"Where are they going to put the seals?" I asked. "On the house?"

"Probably on the doors of the main rooms, which might contain documents or objects of value."

"When is that going to be done?"

"At four o'clock this afternoon. Mademoiselle Jeanne and I have an appointment at Quai Notre Dame with the notary and a magistrate, if I've understood rightly, unless it's someone from the police. I wanted to tell you, in case you want to come, too."

"What's the point?"

"I tried to get in touch with Floriau. Monique told me that he didn't get back for lunch and that he's still at the nursing home, where there appear to be complications . . ."

"What sort?"

"I don't know exactly. Colette obviously can't be forced to stay there against her will. As far as I can gather, she refuses to stay there by herself."

"In other words, she wants to keep Floriau with her?"

"Possibly. It's all complicated by the fact that the medical expert insists that our cousin attend the autopsy and will be waiting for him at three o'clock at the morgue . . ."

"You can say again that it is complicated!" I said, amused.

After a while, I asked:

"Does the notary seem to know what's in the will?"

"At all events, he's taking the thing very seriously. I had the impression that he expected difficulties . . . By the way . . ."

There was a silence.

"What?"

"Nothing . . . She's just made a sign that I shouldn't mention it to you . . . Mother's here."

I should have guessed it. From the moment Lucien was more or less officially placed in charge of the formalities, my mother would hardly even have had lunch before arriving at his apartment.

"Give her my best."

"She wants to know if you've been to the cemetery."

"I'll be going tomorrow morning."

"So you won't be at Quai Notre Dame at four?"

"No! Call me later and tell me what happened."

I hung up. I hadn't turned the light on and my eyes were twitching. I lay down fully dressed on the couch in the living room, opposite the pale window, and dozed off.

Yet I realized where I was, what the time was, and I was aware of Adèle moving about in the kitchen. I remained in the center of the world, of an increasingly blurred world in which my body, the rhythm of my breathing, and my pulse gradually assumed a capital importance.

For some time the image of Colette remained on my retina, the image of a Colette whom I imagined to be naked and, in my torpor, I tried to reconstruct the details of her body.

I could have had her, too, like any other man. If I never tried, it was primarily because I never had the chance, and also for fear of creating complications for myself. It may have been because of Uncle Antoine, too, out of family feeling.

Colette isn't responsible. If a man puts an erotic image before her eyes or simply utters certain evocative words, something is released and she loses control of herself. I talked about her case with a doctor friend of mine (not Floriau, of course), and what he said made me understand a number of things. Above all, it made me understand my uncle's attitude toward his wife.

In the end, my friend said:

"The most worrying part of it all is that, if she is as you say, she may end up by committing suicide."

She had tried to do it the night before, for the third time, apparently, but it was my uncle Antoine who died!

I must have lapsed for a while into a more profound unconsciousness, because, when I opened my eyes, the window was completely dark and dotted with the distant lights of the park. I lay there languidly for a few minutes, my eyes open. As always, I hesitated, out of laziness rather than out of virtue, and I finally pressed the electric bell that rings in the kitchen.

Before Adèle arrived, I switched on the little lamp at the head of the couch, which gives off an orange-colored light. Had Adèle understood already? She took two or three steps into the room, looking for me, and said in her normal voice:

"Oh! you were asleep."

"I slept a little. Get undressed."

She automatically looked around.

"Right away?"

"Yes."

"Here?"

She hadn't yet done it in the living room. I often used to go and see her in her own room, and I had also taken her in ours, when she was making the bed while my wife was out. She never showed any surprise, never said no, and simply watched the door and listened. She had had four successive lovers in less than a year and let herself be taken as naturally as if she were eating. She had no shame, no disgust. For her, a penis was a penis.

"Can you wait just a second? I've got a pot boiling . . ."

She came back a moment later, undoing her white apron.

Then, with the same simplicity, she pulled her black dress over her head.

"Shall I draw the curtains?"

"There's no point. One can't see anything from outside."

I liked to see her undress before the city lights. It wasn't so much that I wanted to make love or to have an orgasm as that I wanted her to undress in the living room. Despite the time I spent at the art school, where we saw models all day long, I have always been obsessed by nakedness, by certain animal postures, as though I were getting back at all the restrictions that had ever been imposed on me.

"Isn't Madame coming back?"

"Not before dinnertime."

Why should I hide from Irène, who wouldn't have objected? I often wondered. There have been a great many Adèles in my life, both at home and outside. I've never mentioned them to anyone. I hide as though I were ashamed.

Well, I'm not. I am not ashamed of my sexual life any more than I am of the rest of my life, but it has to remain secret. Was that the result of the time when I used to go to confession immediately after having had "contact" with a girl, as I used to say?

I could see her standing there, waiting, thickset and white, with heavy breasts and a large black triangle at the base of her belly.

"What shall I do?" she asked.

"Nothing. Not immediately . . ."

She laughed hesitantly.

"Shall I stand here like this?"

"You can sit down . . ."

She sat down, clumsily, on the edge of an armchair. "Like that?"

How many times, during my adolescence, had I dreamed of scenes like this, which then seemed to me to be the height of bliss. Wasn't it because of that memory that I repeated them now?

"What about you?" she asked. "Aren't you going to get undressed?"

No! It wasn't the same thing.

"Can I come closer?"

She couldn't bear keeping still. She joined me on the couch and at that precise moment the front-door bell rang.

"Madame!" exclaimed Adèle, jumping up and rushing over to her scattered clothes. "What shall I do?"

"It's not her. She's got a key. It must be my brother."

Still naked, she ran toward the kitchen and her room, while I went lazily to open the door. I was right. It was Lucien, who brought some of the cold air from outside into the overheated apartment.

He was surprised at the darkness of the hall, at the small lamp alight in the living room, perhaps also at seeing me slightly flushed.

"Were you asleep?" he asked when he saw the cushions in disarray.

"I lay down for a moment after your telephone call and I think I must have fallen asleep. What's the time?"

"Five-thirty. Isn't your wife in?"

"She's gone out."

He probably regretted the question because he must have guessed whom she was with. I'm sure that he pitied me in that moment—he felt pity mingled with an involuntary sense of disgust.

What would he have thought if he'd been in the room a few minutes earlier? Has Lucien ever slept with a woman other than his wife? I doubt it. And yet he doesn't love her. Or at least he didn't love her to begin with. He married her to have a home, children, and to lead a life in accordance with the Scriptures.

The fact is that he used to love—and I would swear that he still loves—Marie Huet, formerly Marie Taboué, who became the wife of Cousin Edouard.

"Is it all over?" I asked, turning on the main light so as to put my brother at ease.

"Yes. It didn't take very long. Together with the notary, Mademoiselle Jeanne went into the library to get the two address books and some files, which she gave to Maître Gauterat. They were both very polite to me, but I felt that I was butting in. There was a third man, a small fair-haired man, to whom I wasn't introduced and who asked François for a candle. He was the one who melted the red wax, stuck the canvas stripe together and affixed the seals . . ."

"On which doors?"

"On the library and our uncle's study, first. And then, after François had had a word under his breath with the notary, on the door of a little safe set in the wall on the second floor, above the bed and hidden behind a picture. It was also François who virtually insisted that the seals be affixed to the cupboards in the pantry that contain the silver. After that we went down to the ground floor, where two of the drawing rooms were closed off."

"Did the notary say anything in particular?"

"He asked for news of Aunt Colette and, when I told him that Floriau had had her taken to the Saint Joseph Nursing Home, he had difficulty in concealing his disapproval. He wanted to know who had been there that morning and which rooms we had gone into . . ."

"Did he mention Edouard?"

"Yes. To inquire about his address. I told him that he's been in town for some days and where he could find him."

"What does that mean?"

"I don't know. He seemed to me slightly worried all the time, just as he had seemed on the telephone. He's a man of few words who answers questions still more dryly than our cousin Floriau. I think that he and Uncle Antoine were great friends.

" 'Did the police say when the body can be picked up?' he asked me.

"I said no and it was to Mademoiselle Jeanne that he gave some instructions, always in an undertone, as though it were none of my business. At a certain point he pulled a diary out of his pocket, consulted it, and then I heard him mention Saturday as the day of the funeral.

" 'We can proceed to the opening of the will in the afternoon,' he added. 'My office will send out the summons . . .'

"As we all stood on the sidewalk outside the house, the notary, his hand on the door of his car, said, 'Mademoiselle Chambovet will keep in touch with you. I assume that she has your telephone number?' "

My brother looked tired, as though he had just had a harassing meeting. I felt he was disappointed by the contempt with which his services were treated, by the limbo into which the family was being cast.

"I managed to ask a last question, all the same," he said, sighing and filling his pipe, the end of which is mended with a piece of wire. "Before the notary closed the door of his car, I asked him if I could arrange for our uncle to have a funeral service. 'It's got nothing to do with me!' he answered dryly. 'Sort that out with the priest.' And he drove off with the secretary."

The Same Day

I dined by myself, and Adèle served me so naturally that one would have thought nothing had happened that afternoon. I didn't even put out my hand to pat her firm bottom. For one thing, my wife could have come back at any moment; it is impossible to tell how long the Sundays at Parantray are going to last. For another, all my lust had vanished. After all, I had had what I wanted.

On any other day, I would have dropped into an armchair with a book in order to savor the tranquility around me while, in town, people were rushing about in spite of the bad weather. But ever since that morning, I had been torn away from my solitude. I suddenly needed to be in contact with people, or at least I needed to know what others were doing at the same time.

I called my cousin Floriau's house and it was Monique who answered. I immediately sensed from her voice, from the way she chose her words, that she was depressed and worried.

"Isn't your husband in?"

"I haven't seen him since this morning. I've only spoken to him on the telephone."

"Was he at the autopsy?"

"Yes. The results were as expected. Uncle Antoine swallowed over twenty barbiturate tablets. On the other hand, although he supposedly had a weak heart for such a long time, it turned out that his heart was in extremely good condition for a man of his age. He could have lived for ten more years."

"And how about Colette?"

At this point, Monique's voice dropped very low and she spoke with hesitancy.

"It appears that she suddenly grew very calm and reasonable. The psychiatrist, who is a friend of Jean's, doesn't know what to do, since he has no right to keep her there by force in her present state. Nor has he any right to make her undergo a cure, which might diminish her lucidity, without her consent. She's pretty shrewd!"

There was a note of bitterness in the voice of Monique, who was usually so serene in her role as an exemplary wife, mother, and hostess. Did she sense that her marriage was threatened?

"Is she going home?"

"She may already be there. I know that Jean doesn't trust this apparent calmness. He's had to get two nurses to take turns looking after her on Quai Notre Dame. What I ask myself is whether she'll let him leave . . ."

Irène came in at that moment in a sulky and aggressive mood, so I had to hang up.

"Well? Is it the inheritance? Have the Huets lost it?"

"The will is going to be opened only after the funeral."

She threw her coat onto one armchair and sank into another, stretching her legs out in front of the fire.

"Well, I who am what one might call an interested party would find it simply disgusting if we got this inheritance that everybody has been talking about. However mad, however hysterical, Colette gave that man the happiest years of his life and I don't see why you and your family should inherit. . . ."

I didn't go on about it. I didn't ask her why she was in such a bad temper. She went to put on her dressing gown. We both read for a while, sitting at opposite ends of the room, she a magazine, I a book of memoirs, and we went to bed at about eleven.

"Not tonight, if you don't mind," she said, moving away from me.

The next morning, All Souls' Day, I got up before she did, as usual, and she was still asleep, or pretended to be, when I left the house at half past nine. This time I remembered to take the car keys. I drove out of the garage and up to the embankment. The town had regained part of its customary appearance, although certain shops and offices were closed. People carrying flowers could still be seen hurrying to the cemetery.

I drove past Quai Notre Dame on purpose, in order to glance once more at my uncle's house.

I was surprised to see an undertaker's van parked outside the carriage door, which was thrown wide open. François, dressed in black with his white four-in-hand tie and his bald pate, stood beneath the archway while two men were unloading huge bales of black drapery.

Who had organized everything so quickly? The notary, Mademoiselle Jeanne, or my brother? Whoever it was, I could see that they were going to set up a mortuary chapel in the house.

I made for the cemetery. The rain was pouring onto my windshield so heavily that the wipers occasionally hesitated. I had an umbrella. I bought a chrysanthemum plant at the gate and started down one of the paths covered with dead leaves.

There were women, some of whom held one or two children by the hand, and very few men wandering among the dilapidated tombs; I saw an old woman, bent with age, digging the earth at the foot of a wooden cross, which was undoubtedly temporarily set up.

The cemetery has been enlarged recently and I had some difficulty finding my father's tomb, with the dates 1893–1943 underneath his name. The grave is well kept up. I added my flowers to the ones that were already there, wedged the pot in with a stone, and stood for a moment in meditation.

I was just about to leave when I recognized Marie, my cousin Edouard's wife, a few yards away from me.

She was standing beneath her umbrella, in front of a tomb that meant nothing to her, a pretentious monument of pink marble. She turned toward me and, when my eyes met hers, she came forward gallantly.

That is the right word for her. Marie, whom I always want to call by her maiden name, Marie Taboué, is a gallant girl who faces up to life, simply, modestly, and who accepts fate, whatever it may be, without flinching.

God knows that she has every reason to complain! Her face is clear, everything about her is clear. With her blue coat and blue hat with a white border, she looked a little like a nurse, although she only works as a hospital receptionist.

"Hello, Blaise. Your mother told me you'd be here this morning early. Since I had to visit my parents' grave, I waited for you."

"Isn't your son with you?"

It was hard to believe from her young, almost virginal appearance that she had a son sixteen and a half, Philippe, who had just passed his final exam with flying colors and had got into the university.

"I'd like to have a word with you. Do you mind my having waited for you?"

I knew what she was going to talk about and it was probably going to take some time. We couldn't really discuss such a topic pacing the cemetery under our umbrellas.

"We'd better shelter somewhere."

We decided on one of the two cafés opposite the main gate. A few men were having a drink and some women had brought a snack with them and were eating it in front of cups of coffee. There were rivulets of water on the floor; it was drafty and there was a stale smell of faded flowers and wet earth.

Seated in a peaceful corner, next to a couple of anonymous peasants, we ordered coffee and then, when it came, we remained silent for a while.

"I gather you saw Lucien yesterday. Your mother saw him, too, but she hardly had a chance to talk to him. Did he say anything to you?"

I shook my head, conveying the truth, since I had no idea of my brother's real reactions.

"He knows, doesn't he?"

"Yes."

"He knows he's staying with me, too?"

"He's found out."

"I'd like you to talk to him, Blaise, and get this wretched business over with. I can understand your brother. I can understand the attitude of the family. And now Uncle Antoine's death has complicated matters still further!"

She was upset and her pretty breasts, round and firm, held in strictly by a tight brassiere, moved with her rapid respiration. She was not crying.

"If only you could see what a state he's in!"

"I can understand that you feel pity for him," I murmured.

It was silly of me. I should have realized that the word would hurt her, but she reacted far more violently than I would ever have expected from her. She said, almost dryly:

"I would rather you never used the term pity to

describe any feeling of mine. I may be asking the rest of you for pity, and especially Lucien, who has more cause than anyone else to have it in for Edouard. But as for me, he's my husband. He's Philippe's father. He's the only man I ever loved and I still love him."

Her voice broke on the last words and she looked away for a moment. I wanted to touch her bare hand to show her that I understood.

"Edouard is in the wrong, that's obvious," she went on, pulling herself together, "and I'm not trying to defend him. But is it right that there should be no end to his punishment? He's now thirty-eight years old, but in fact he's ageless. When I saw him standing on the sidewalk three days ago, gazing at the house . . ."

She took her handkerchief out of her bag and bit on it in order to control herself, in order not to burst into tears, and this time I reached out for her hand fraternally.

"Look, Blaise!" she went on, breathlessly, leaning toward me because of the couple sitting next to us, who were now trying to hear what we were saying. "You know Edouard. You remember what he was like in his youth, the best looking and the proudest of the lot of you. He was arrogant about it and it was as though the world belonged to him. Well, the man lurking around my house the other day was a wreck. He was like a starving dog nosing the garbage cans . . .

"I knew that he was in town. I heard that he had been seen in one of those derelict areas near the canal where foreign workers sleep five or six to a room . . .

"I wondered whether he would have the courage to appear at my house. I both wanted him to and didn't want him to, because of Philippe . . . I thought of sending him a message or some money . . . but how?

"I stood behind the curtain looking at him shivering in the cold, bent, diminished, and humiliated, and when he looked up at the window I couldn't resist. I rushed down the stairs, opened the door and beckoned to him.

"He hesitated before crossing the street. Finally, he came into the hall without looking me in the face and suddenly, the door still open, I fell into his arms weeping. . . ."

Marie's hand was cold in mine. She was still not crying, and simply sniffed.

"He's ill, like his father, like yours. He sometimes has two attacks a day and sits motionless, staring into space, unable to make a single movement. You remember your father, don't you? Only he was forty-five when that started. Edouard also has stomach trouble and can't hold down anything he eats . . .

"I almost went to see Lucien. Then I thought it might embarrass him. He's always been very good to me. He never held anything against me. It was he who helped me get my job at the hospital, and Philippe regards him almost as a father . . .

"I can't let him go away again, Blaise! You see, he's at the end of his tether. You know him well enough to know that if he had the inkling of a hope left he wouldn't have humiliated himself by coming back here. . . ."

I wasn't as sure as she was. Edouard is pretty good at pretending and this wasn't the first time that he's promised to change his life. Personally, I don't feel any hostility toward him. As for Lucien, I'm sure that he's forgiven him like a good Christian. But might he not try to defend Marie against herself and against her husband?

"For the time being, he's lying low, he's hiding, he refuses to go out."

"What's he frightened of?"

"I don't think it's fear. It may be shame. He knows what you all think of him. He wonders what would happen if he met one of you, especially Lucien, in the street. He wants to work because he doesn't intend to sponge on me . . ."

"What does he propose to do?"

Edouard had no training and never had a proper job in his life. All he had ever done is to swindle people.

"He'd do anything. He admitted to me that he worked as a sandwich man in London and that some evenings he opened car doors at the entrance to a music hall."

Yet Marie was right: in his youth he had been the best looking, the most daring, and the most promising of us all. He's the only dark-haired one in our family, with wavy hair, deep-blue eyes, and the proud features of a Greek statue.

He was gifted and enterprising and nobody could resist him. Not only were women seduced by him: even men would be enchanted by his aggressive vitality. At the age of twenty he was a wild young man with flashing teeth, and while we still paced the streets elaborating nebulous planes, he founded a review and managed to find the backers necessary for setting up a private printing press.

The war was on, not our parents' war but the 1939 war, and the occupation. We lived in slow motion, as it were, with a weight on our shoulders, a terror of the future, the constant worry about food, the fear of being deported.

Of all the family, of all our friends, Edouard alone lived as though the future belonged to him. Well dressed and handsome, he used to go to black-market restaurants, arm in arm with beautiful women, while his sister, Monique, who wasn't married and hadn't yet met Floriau, spent her time working in the local soup kitchen.

My parents and I lived in a different neighborhood from that of Edouard, his mother, and Monique. My father, who was already ill, was to die in 1943, the year when my brother was deported and when, for two months, everyone thought he was going to be shot.

I was lucky enough not to be taken prisoner when the armistice was signed and I was fighting in Alsace, so I managed to return home. That was the time when I had given up studying architecture and worked with my father, doing drawings for a publicity agency.

Lucien, who gave out ration cards at the town hall, was rather mysterious and it was only after the Liberation that we discovered he had been working for the Resistance.

Marie Taboué lived next door to us. She was the daughter of a widowed schoolmaster, and she did all the housework as well as bring up her younger brother, who was to die later in a car crash.

She was then as she was now, sitting in front of me in the restaurant near the cemetery—or, rather, she hadn't changed; she was just as fresh, as straight, as touching.

I think I may well have been slightly in love with her myself.

When he was nineteen, and although he was two years younger than she, Lucien had decided to marry her. My parents and I knew nothing about this. My brother has always been secretive, out of modesty.

But Marie Taboué did know, and she hadn't said no to him.

On the morning of All Souls' Day, in that café usually frequented by funeral parties, she simply said:

"I loved Lucien as a brother. I didn't dare discourage him, because I respected him too much to make him unhappy. Perhaps, if I hadn't met Edouard, I might have married him, and that would have been better for everybody."

It was at my parents' house, at home, as I used to say in those days, that she met Edouard, and I still wonder how this meeting can have taken place, since my cousin didn't see very much of us. For some reason or other, maybe because we all had problems of our own, the family bonds slackened during the war and I can hardly remember the few encounters with my aunts and uncles.

Admittedly, I myself participated very little in family life. That's the darkest, emptiest, most anguished period of my existence and I never think about it without distaste. I could see no future for myself and I hadn't yet resigned myself to that fact.

The bitingly pessimistic philosophy of my friend Denèvre, whom I saw almost every evening, gradually started to wash off on me. If he despised men, he was still harder on women. He really hated them and, at about nine o'clock on Saturday evening, he used to look at his watch and say:

"Well, it's sewer time."

He didn't have any permanent affair and simply went once a week to a quiet prostitute named Zulma, who was almost the same age as my mother. She lived in a ground-floor apartment on a middle-class street and she kept it remarkably clean, obliging her visitors to put on felt slippers in order not to sully the polished parquet floor. She had red hair, pale, soft skin, and a pretty smile. I went to her a couple of times, too.

"Is your friend like that with everyone?"

Apparently, he was extremely vulgar with her and intentionally used the coarsest language.

However much I lived at home, I was no longer really part of it. I had never been on very close terms with my brother, who was three years younger than I. It would never have occurred to me to confide in my mother, even as a child, and the world of my aunts and uncles seemed to be positively nightmarish.

That was the last year of my father's life. We all knew it. I spent several hours a day working with him in his studio. But I never once worried about what he was thinking. He didn't ask me any questions, either; or if he did, they were of the vague kind, which I answered still more vaguely. So today I still wonder what sort of a man he really was.

Nearly all I know about that period comes from my mother.

It is consequently secondhand information and I have to take into account the inevitable deformation she has imposed on it.

Why, on that day, when Marie Taboué was at our house, as happened frequently since we were neighbors, why, I repeat, did my cousin Edouard, who lived in such a different world, decide to bring us two pounds of butter?

It's not the gesture that amazes me, it's the coincidence, and, above all, the consequences. The gesture was typical of him. He could be unexpectedly kind, gratuitously attentive.

I remember that on that day my mother was preparing some jam (without sugar!) and Marie Taboué was helping her, covering the jars with disks of transparent paper soaked in brandy. So it must have been in July or August toward evening, because the sun was streaming obliquely into the kitchen.

I didn't stay and I now regret it; I would have witnessed the impact that Edouard made on our little neighbor. She told Lucien later that she had loved Edouard ever since that first moment and that her only thought had been to see him again.

The unfortunate thing is that she didn't tell my cousin. She was still struggling against herself and she led him to believe that she was engaged to Lucien.

Anyhow, over a certain period of time Edouard came to the house frequently, nearly always bringing some sort of food. He had a plan about which I knew only the broad outlines from others, since he never confided in me.

Ever since the beginning of the occupation, *Le Nouvelliste*, the only paper in town, had been scuttled, as we used to say. It was a conservative, old-fashioned-looking paper that had been run before the war by two or three editors who had grown gray in the service.

Edouard, who had a printing press and was already publishing a small review, was thinking of the post-war future and planning an up-to-date paper that was to compete with *Le Nouvelliste* and perhaps even prevent it from reappearing.

He had found some support for his scheme, a fact that gives an idea of his enterprise at the time, since he was only just twenty-four. My mother claims that Uncle Antoine himself backed him and had vouched for him before several local authorities.

But, quite suddenly, in September, several weeks after the episode of the butter, and consequently after the meeting between Marie Taboué and Edouard, the German police burst into our house, searched it from cellar to attic and, after pushing my father around brutally, went off with Lucien.

That same day six other people who were in touch with my brother were arrested, including a radio vender on Rue Poincaré who was later to be shot.

Having heard nothing for a month, we were then told that my brother and his companions were in Buchenwald concentration camp.

Did this episode hasten my father's death? Possibly. He died in his studio three days after hearing the news, so Lucien never saw him again.

Within six months Edouard had married Marie Taboué. My mother implied that she was pregnant and she must have been right, since Philippe was born well before the normal time.

We didn't tell Lucien, from whom we received very little news, and that nearly always indirectly. We were awaiting the attack announced by Radio London. Notices were put up to arrange for the departure of all able-bodied men for Germany, so we fluctuated between hope and terror.

There was a time when I spent every night in the house of a friend of my mother's who had a little farm about two miles out of town, beyond the Bois de La Barraude. I went there by bicycle, making a detour in order to avoid the checkpoint at the grade crossing.

The Allies disembarked, Paris was liberated, and then

came our turn. Edouard lived with his wife and baby in the house he had rented not far from us and where Marie and Philippe still live.

Why did he disappear overnight? Admittedly, the marriage hadn't made him any less of a womanizer. He often spent his evenings and part of his nights in a little nightclub, the only one open at the time. It had a somewhat shady clientele, and, according to rumor, he had fallen in love with a Parisian singer known as Choupette.

I am always amazed when I think of the quantity and variety of information collected by my mother about every member of the family. Whomever one mentions to her, she seems to know about their most intimate behavior.

And it isn't simply gossip—I soon realized that. She says fairly little about what she knows and only reveals it when she wants to, for a definite reason.

I think that is because my mother has what one might call a sense of calamity. She senses disaster from afar and, as soon as something disagreeable happens to somebody, she is sure to appear, as she appeared in my apartment on that morning of Allhallows.

It is she, too, who is ready to take on any awkward or embarrassing task, who looks after a sick child or does the housework for a bedridden relation or neighbor.

Even if one doesn't tell her anything, she never takes long to discover the truth, or what she considers to be the truth.

With regard to Edouard and his wife, she said, right at the beginning:

"The marriage won't last. Marie is too straightforward, too simple. It's because of her simplicity that she gave him what he wanted, without realizing that, for him, it was a mere whim."

Anyhow, my cousin left town one fine evening at the same time as Choupette and, months later, he was seen in Paris.

It was at that moment that rumors started to circulate. Even the Purification Committee, which was formed immediately after the Germans left, was told about him. It was almost certain that Edouard had gone in for black-marketeering on a very large scale, but what astonished everybody was his impunity. Even if he had never been seen with the Germans, it was nevertheless rumored that he had had secret dealings with them.

Admittedly, the same thing was said about people who were perfectly innocent and many were arrested. Women who had had nothing to do with the whole business had their heads shaved.

What is certain is that, after my cousin's departure, it emerged that he owed money right and left and that he had gone off with the funds of his backers. Why didn't they sue him? All I can say is that in the whole of this period I took no notice of others and that the family was the last of my problems.

Lucien returned from Germany, emaciated, in bad health, and for two months he couldn't eat a normal meal because his stomach was so unaccustomed to food.

Of course, he heard that Marie had married in his

absence, that she had a child, and that Edouard had left town.

He didn't confide in me. Thanks to Uncle Antoine, he got a job at *Le Nouvelliste* and we hardly saw him at home any more.

It was a friend of our father's, a certain Lautrade who worked at the prefecture, who found the letter. He had been ordered to sort out the mountains of papers the Germans had left behind at their headquarters. After several weeks he came across an anonymous letter denouncing Lucien as a member of the Resistance.

Because of that letter my brother was followed without his knowing it for several days, hence the arrests made the same day as his own.

When he saw the letter, my brother immediately recognized Edouard's handwriting. For once he confided in me, because he was afraid of being wrong. We compared the note with other samples of my cousin's handwriting and there was no possible doubt.

Now, opposite the cemetery, Marie said to me, her hands clasped in supplication:

"One can't pay all one's life, Blaise! There comes a time when . . . Can you talk to Lucien? If he wants, I'll go and see him . . . I'll repeat what I've just said to you . . . I'll go on my knees to him . . ."

"It wasn't only Lucien . . ."

How did it get around? Through my mother? Did Lautrade talk? Anyhow, the whole family and a good part of the town has known about it for years.

"If Lucien forgives him, I'm sure the others won't dare . . ."

She clasped her hands so tightly that her fingers went white.

"Are you going to continue to live together?" I asked.

"He's my husband."

"What does Philippe say?"

"He doesn't know his father. He's never seen him. I've told him he's ill, in a room on the second floor, and it's true, because I forced Edouard to go to bed."

"Doesn't your son know anything?"

"People have spoken to him, of course. He's afraid for me. Afraid that his father will hurt me. I wonder if he's not slightly jealous, too. But I'll take care of that. It's Lucien and the others who frighten me. In a day or two I'll introduce Philippe to his father. I'll prepare him for it . . ."

"Does he know that he's been to prison?"

"He's been told."

The whole town knows about that. Ever since his departure Edouard has lived not only in Paris, but also in Marseilles, Algiers, Brussels, and God knows where else. From time to time his wife received heartbroken letters in which he said that, for a lack of a certain sum that he had to pay back at all costs, he had no alternative but to commit suicide.

Lucien read these letters because, although he married Thérèse Bourdillat, a childhood friend, a few years later, he remained Marie's confidant and moral support.

He often goes to see her, as one might go to see a sister, and he takes great interest in Philippe's studies.

Was it against his advice that Marie sent Edouard money each time he asked for it? My mother received similar letters, one of which, written by a so-called nurse, said that Edouard was in a hospital—in Algiers, as far as I can remember—and that he was completely destitute.

Like Marie, my mother sent him a check, and she says that Uncle Antoine came repeatedly to my cousin's assistance.

On various occasions during these sixteen years it has been rumored that he was in town. Some people had seen him looking marvelous and talking about fantastic business deals he was about to bring off, while others had seen him shabbily dressed and begging for a thousand-franc note.

I took advantage of a pause to ask Marie:

"Is it true that this isn't the first time he's come back?"

"He came back once, ten years ago. He waited for me at the door of the hospital where I work."

"Did he ask you for money?"

She simply batted her eyelashes.

In England, where he lived with a notorious prostitute, he was arrested for pimping. If I know him, it's perfectly possible that he was in love with the woman, whose photograph I saw in the papers and who was very beautiful. It is also quite probable that he lived off her, or that, at least, is what the English law thought, since he was sentenced to two years in prison.

Were there some highlights in this existence of which I

know only the squalor? Probably, for, in spite of everything, Edouard is resourceful.

"So," I said to Marie, "you want Lucien to go and see him?"

"That would be a help, especially as far as Philippe is concerned. For my son, Lucien is God Almighty, and if he sees him shake his father's hand . . ."

"I'll talk to him," I promised.

As I was signaling to the waiter she grabbed my arm.

"Just a minute," she murmured in embarrassment. "That's not all. I thought that on Saturday . . ."

Le Nouvelliste that morning had announced that my uncle's funeral service would be held in the cathedral on Saturday morning at ten o'clock. As I expected, the paper didn't mention suicide but "an overdose of barbiturates." So people could believe that his death had been accidental.

"The whole family will be there," Marie went on, not daring to look me in the eye. "Everyone knows my husband is in town. Uncle Antoine was always lenient with him. That would be the time . . ."

"Edouard put that idea into your head, didn't he?"

She had to say yes. She was unable to lie. Besides, that was so typical of Edouard! He came back emaciated, ill, an animal crawling back to its lair. He appeared humble and repentant before his wife. She welcomed him, put him in clean sheets, and before he had even made peace with his own son, he was working out a sort of family acceptance.

Edouard at the funeral, pale, probably in a new suit—that would wipe out his past and would signify his reintegration not only into his home and family, but also in the township.

I couldn't help sighing as I looked at her in admiration.

"My poor Marie . . ."

She was intelligent enough to know the part her husband wanted her to play and she was playing it as best she could. Didn't she see, as I did, that if she succeeded it would start all over again? Did she have any idea of what her life would be like with her son and this husband who had abandoned them for sixteen years and who had only temporarily been changed by misery?

"You mustn't be sorry for me," she replied, trying to smile courageously. "I told you: I've always only loved him . . . I still love him . . ."

The words passed through her tight throat with difficulty.

"Come along!" I said, handing her her bag and umbrella.

I added reluctantly:

"I'll try."

Of course, Marie hasn't got a car. There aren't many cars in the family and, were it not for my wife, I wouldn't have one, either. Maybe if I saved up long enough I would be able to buy myself a motor scooter.

"I'll drive you back," I said, once we were in the street.

"I can take the streetcar, Blaise. Don't go out of your way for me."

"Get in!"

That meant that I returned, in the blinding rain, to the part of town where I lived as a child, and I wonder why I feel a kind of unease, of anguish, every time, as though I were again about to be imprisoned in that network of abnormally quiet streets, with only a rare walker here and there, an old woman cautiously opening her door, a curtain moving.

We used to live on Rue des Vergers. When Marie left her father in order to get married, she had only to go around the corner and walk three hundred yards: Rue des

Saules, where she has been living for sixteen years, is exactly the same as the street where she was born.

Why does everything in that area seem immobile to me, not only the houses, the windows, but also the benches and the elms in the square, even the people, who appear to go through the same motions as they did when I used to live there?

Everything has grown old. The façades, freshly painted when I was a child, have acquired a patina. Houses that I saw being built look obsolete. And the people living in them who were the same age as my father and mother, are now old men and women.

When all the old people are dead, there must be some young ones to replace them, unless they tear the whole neighborhood down and rebuild it. They have thought of doing it. My father had known that part of town when there were real orchards and real willows, which gave their name to certain streets, and, when I was born, there was a last farm, with cows, chickens, and pigs, bordering on the canal.

I made a detour in order to avoid the street where I used to live. I stopped in front of Marie's house and automatically raised my eyes to the windows on the second floor. I couldn't see any shadow behind them.

"Thanks, Blaise. I count on you."

She had wanted to return home calm, and she managed to do so.

"I'll do the best I can."

"Thanks."

She crossed the sidewalk running, the key in her hand, while I started the car.

When I got home I found Irène in a dressing gown.

"Did you go to the cemetery? Did you see your mother?"

"No. Why?"

"Nothing."

Stretched out on the couch in the drawing room, my wife was filing her nails, while Adèle set the table in the next room. Irène liked to hang around the apartment in a negligée, slippers on her bare feet, her hair loose, not doing anything in particular, and when I get home from the Academy I'm sometimes surprised to find her exactly as I had left her three hours earlier.

Her behavior, her tastes, and her language have remained rather vulgar, but I don't mind that. On the contrary, I wanted it that way. I could never have lived with a woman like my cousin Monique, or even like Marie, who, without wanting to, would have given me a feeling of inferiority.

I would be going too far to say that I chose my wife, deliberately, on the lowest possible level, almost in the gutter; one never really chooses. Yet she is the only type of woman I could ever marry, a woman who does not exert any restriction on me or force me into any competition.

Her mother, old Fernande, used to wheel a vegetable cart through the streets. With her blotchy complexion, her enormous hips, her raucous voice, she sat with the men at the bar drinking copiously. She died in the hospital, during an attack of delirium tremens, like any old drunkard.

She had two daughters. When I met Irène she was working in a flower shop on Rue de la Poste. Her sister was four years younger, and I admit that I hesitated between the two, and very nearly married Lili. I didn't, however, because she was only sixteen at the time.

She left town shortly afterward and as far as I know has never been back. During her first three years in Paris we heard nothing about her. Then we received a notification of her marriage to an impresario named Block.

They had a child, a little girl, but that didn't keep her from divorcing him four years later and marrying again.

Her second husband is an Englishman, Harry Higgins, from the brewing family. They have an apartment in Paris, another in London, a large estate in Sussex, a villa on the Riviera. Their name crops up in the society columns whenever there's a gala performance in Cannes or Monte Carlo.

Irène, poor creature, was less lucky with me. It has to be admitted, though, that her sister had a sparkle, an exuberance, sheer animal spirits which Irène never did match.

"Give me a glass of port, Blaise, will you? I've almost finished. Only two nails left."

What I appreciate most is that we are at ease with each other. I'm just as natural with her as I would be with a male friend, as I was with Denèvre, for instance.

Since we know each other so well we make no attempt

to hide our faults, still less to correct each other. That's what's so restful about it and what most people can't understand.

She had that concentrated look she has whenever she takes care of her body, whether it's polishing her nails, putting on make-up, or brushing her hair. One feels that this is her essential task and she can spend hours at it without ever getting bored, with the radio on in the background, occasionally pausing to light a cigarette.

I poured myself a glass of port, too. When I gave her hers our eyes met peaceably. And when she spoke I knew what she had been thinking about all morning.

"What would you do," she asked, "if you were to inherit?"

I hadn't thought about it that morning, because of Marie, but I had the night before, just as I was dropping off to sleep, and I hadn't come up with an answer.

"That depends."

I sat down in front of her, my glass in my hand.

"It depends on what?"

"To start with, on how much."

"Do you think he was very rich?"

I knew that Irène wasn't saying all this out of greed and that her questions were prompted by a distant past.

"I wouldn't know whether he was very rich. But the house on Quai Notre Dame alone must be worth about forty million. He certainy had securities. My mother claims that he owned some other buildings. Only, a large sum shared between all the Huets . . ."

"Of course!" She sighed.

Did that mean that she was getting bored with Nicolas Macherin? In any case, I liked that sigh; it gave me an agreeable sensation.

Contrary to what people think, I love my wife and I believe that she loves me. In her own way, no doubt. But she couldn't do without me. The proof is that she didn't do as her sister did and that she has stayed with me.

Of course, Nicolas would never marry her. I have had occasion to observe him for three years and he makes no attempt to hide his views on the subject. He has no desire to complicate his life with a wife, a household, and children. As for mistresses, he had one once who fleeced him and almost involved him in a scandal.

His sexual requirements are moderate, his curiosity has long been dulled. He enjoys his solitary bachelor life. But he still needs a place where, whenever he wants and only when he wants, he can find something resembling the warmth of a home.

I know that my mother regards him as a cuckoo, and she's not altogether wrong. My presence at table when he comes to lunch or dinner doesn't bother him. On the contrary, I feel sure that it would bore him to have to stay for too long alone with Irène and not feel a real family around him.

Even Lucien must be convinced that I have accepted out of self-interest what he calls a false situation. Nothing is further from the truth, but I never took the trouble to explain the matter to him, or to anyone else.

Irene was unfaithful to me before she met Macherin. When I met her I was well aware that she attached no importance to sexual acts, which seemed to her just as humdrum and natural as they did to someone like Adèle. Several of my friends slept with her before I did, and that didn't stop me from marrying her.

That doesn't mean that I wasn't jealous. I admit that I hoped her attitude would change. But I loved her for her faults, not for her virtues, and I certainly wasn't the man to reform her.

The strangest thing is that she is not at all oversexed, and I'm sure that she has never really known sexual pleasure. She enjoys the sexual act occasionally, but most of the time it's either the inevitable end of an evening or a means of paying her way.

She's not ambitious in any true sense of the word and she doesn't envy her sister, whose opulent way of life and responsibilities would probably scare her.

No! It's something different. When she gets bored she needs noise, lights; she needs to laugh with someone who is looking after her and who makes her believe in her own importance. It doesn't matter if she has to end up in bed! She doesn't think of it in advance, and when the time comes she does what she has to do.

It seems to me that no husband is capable of giving her this and the proof is that she deceived me, to use a word that I regard as inaccurate, within a month of our marriage.

At the time, she didn't talk about it and felt she ought to hide. Consequently, she became entangled in lies.

One day when she came back with a new handbag, which I knew she couldn't afford, I realized what was happening.

I could have been angry or preached to her or hit her. Should I have? Would people now look at me less disapprovingly? Or, since it was impossible to change her, should I have divorced her, although I felt incapable of living without her?

I described all this in detail in the manuscript I had destroyed, trying to analyze the various stages through which I passed. But I was led to believe that it was in bad taste, that it was a product of exhibitionism.

Is it now more obvious why I always took a particular interest in my uncle Antoine? His situation was not quite the same as mine, but there are nevertheless certain points in common in our respective attitudes.

Colette isn't off the street like Irène. She comes from an excellent family from the south, from Nîmes, I believe, and she is well brought up.

Antoine Huet met her on the Riviera, where he stayed every year and where she lived with her mother.

How did a man who was thirty years older than she was persuade her to come and live in our misty town? Nobody in the family knows anything about this.

What I would swear, from personal experience, is that my uncle knew she was a nymphomaniac and would make him suffer. Unlike Irène, she didn't go with men because she attached no importance to it or to pay for her dinner or for an evening in a nightclub or for some trifling piece of jewelry. To Colette it was a major event every time, which made her suffer profoundly.

Had she not married a man old enough to be her father in the hope that he would save her? He understood her. He helped her. I'm sure that it was thanks to him and his sympathetic attitude that she could lead an almost normal existence in spite of everything. In a sense he acted as a psychiatric nurse.

Antoine, like me, must have spent entire evenings and nights wondering whether she would come back this time. He must have started at the sound of the door, of her steps on the stairs, trying to retain a serene expression on his face.

Unlike me, however, he hoped to cure her. I only cherished that hope for a few months or, rather, a few weeks.

"Again, Irène?" I would say to begin with, in a rather muffled voice.

"What? What have I done? What are you cross about?"

"You know, don't you?"

Sometimes she got angry and rebelled.

"If it was to shut me between four walls and make me wait for you all day you shouldn't have married me."

What could I say to that? She was right and I became gentler, tenderer toward her. I tried to be gay, to take her to places she liked. She knew I didn't feel at ease in them. She knew me too well.

And besides! I must add that she wanted to have everything she saw. To start with, she wanted a maid because she hated to do the housework. Who did the housework in her own home? Nobody, probably. They lived in an easygoing manner, in a sort of hovel, eating what came to hand, usually some cold cuts, at the kitchen table.

Was I going to teach her to cook, to make the bed, to keep within a modest budget? I tried, in my simple-minded way. For years I did the washing up when I came home and counted the linen for the laundry.

I love her. I love her little face, so easily turning sulky, and I also love her body, even if she yields it to me indifferently. I love her laziness, her shiftlessness, her almost animal or infantile way of living. I need to know that she's there, that I can go home to her or wait for her, guess at her mood from a twist of her lips.

Whatever people say, we are a couple, despite Macherin and the others, and if I accepted Macherin, if I ended up by getting used to him, it was in order not to lose her.

She needed a car, a fur coat, all the rather vulgar luxury of a kept woman that makes her feel in her element.

The night before, in bed, listening to her regular breathing, I, too, had asked myself:

"And what if I really inherited?"

For a moment I basked in illusions. Would I not have Irène all to myself at last?

I tried to imagine us on our own together, without my classes at the Academy, alone together almost every hour of the day, and I realized that my wife wouldn't stand it.

I wonder whether Nicolas isn't as necessary to her as I am, in a different sense. Because of his age, his fortune, his social importance, he represents authority for her. Without going so far as to say that she's afraid of him, he certainly impresses her. She gets cross with him just as she would with a father, if she had one.

I have had occasion to watch these subterranean rebellions, which amuse Nicolas and which he enjoys provoking.

He constitutes a break, even if Irène feels the need to be unfaithful to him. But I no longer act as a break in any way. I am the companion, almost the accomplice, the man she is sure to find, whatever happens, and who she knows will ask no questions and will understand without appearing to understand.

"It would be funny if we suddenly became rich!"

And I felt that it worried her, that it wasn't a purely pleasant prospect, that for her, too, it presented some insoluble problems.

"Lunch is served, madame," said Adèle in her indifferent tone of voice.

When I telephoned my brother, shortly after lunch, his wife said that he was at the paper.

"Are you using the car?" I asked Irène.

She looked at the rain pouring down the windowpanes and sighed.

"I may go to the movies. What else can one do on a day like this?"

I took the streetcar. On Rue Vineuse I went into the old-fashioned, ill-lighted lobby of *Le Nouvelliste* with its two windows, one with the inscription ADVERTISEMENTS, the other marked SUBSCRIPTIONS. In the display cases set against two walls, among marching armies and heads of state stepping out of airplanes, I noticed photographs of my uncle taken on various occasions of official ceremonies.

On the front page of the paper there was also a portrait of him and three columns of obituary signed by the editor.

It is difficult to find my brother's office, which is near the composing room. First one has to go along several narrow corridors, then up a staircase, and through rooms crowded with stacks of old newspapers. I only came across one secretary, who had a squint and pointed to the composing room from behind a partition.

There was Lucien in his shirt sleeves, leaning over the forms with the compositor. The linotypes were clicking away and there was a strong smell of molten lead. I'd never seen Lucien with glasses on. I didn't know that he wore them at work, an old-fashioned model with steel rims. He greeted me in surprise, almost uneasily.

"Do you want to talk to me?"

"I've got plenty of time."

"I'll be with you in ten minutes. You can wait in my office."

I preferred to wander around the composing room. That's Lucien's realm, just as the classroom at the Academy, with its pale marble and the students in their coveralls, is mine. I was amazed to see him read the lead lines back to front and, with an adroit movement, remove and replace them with his pincers.

Here, for those who worked with him, Lucien was quite somebody. Everyone recognized his professionalism, his ability. That made me gloomy. Doesn't everyone have to feel his own importance in some domain or other, no matter how humble? I never had this satisfaction. My students don't take me seriously and make faces behind my back. The other teachers are well aware that I owe my job to protection. My family, including my mother, despises me or pities me, and the only person for whom I count at all is Irène.

Or perhaps I count a great deal for her? She would undoubtedly be dismayed if I disappeared. But it wouldn't be real despair. Just a while ago, as we were having lunch, she pointed to the paper announcing my uncle's funeral and asked me:

"Do you think I should wear mourning? I haven't got a black coat."

"You can wear your mink."

"I bet your mother and your aunts will wear a veil."

I felt that she was tempted to wear one too, to see if it suited her, as though she were putting on a disguise.

I followed Lucien into his office, where he appeared to wait for me to start speaking. I pointed to the secretary and he hesitated to send her out.

"Let's go and have a coffee across the street," he said in the end, putting on his jacket. "If anyone asks for me, Geneviève, say that I'll be back shortly."

The old-fashioned café, with its imitation-leather seats and the mirrors lining both rooms, is a café for habitués where I can't remember ever having set foot before. It was almost empty. Two men in shirt sleeves were moving slowly and solemnly around a billiard table and one of them, a police inspector, came up to shake my brother's hand. My brother ordered a coffee. I'd had one at home, so I asked for a brandy, which seemed to surprise Lucien.

Curious and ill at ease, he looked at me as though he were trying to guess the purpose of my unexpected visit.

As soon as we were alone I took the plunge.

"I saw Marie."

He expected it.

"Did she go to your apartment?"

"No. I met her this morning at the cemetery."

"With Philippe?"

"She was alone."

He had already understood that it was not a chance meeting, for he knew Marie and her habits far better than I did.

"Why did she turn to you?" he asked with a touch of bitterness.

"Because she didn't dare go to you."

"Does she know you're here? Did she send you?"

"Yes."

There was a silence during which we could hear the billiard balls colliding under the green-shaded lamp over the table.

"What did she want you to tell me?"

I have rarely felt how different my brother and I are. Even his voice, which I had heard every day throughout his youth, sounded to me like the voice of a stranger. I looked at him and didn't recognize any of my own features. He remained outwardly calm. His agitation, if it existed, was within.

"You know that he's staying with her, don't you?"

"Yes."

"It appears that he's very ill, that he's only a shadow of himself."

His fingers drummed on the table and I noticed tufts of red hair on each joint.

"So?" he asked.

"She's put him to bed in a room on the second floor."

"How about Philippe?"

"Philippe hasn't seen him yet."

"Does he know?"

"Yes."

"How did he react?"

"She wants him to get used to the idea little by little . . ."

"To what idea?"

"That his father is back."

"Does she propose to keep him?"

"Look, Lucien, your way of asking questions doesn't make things easier for me. I promised Marie I'd plead for her."

"At the cemetery?"

"In a café just opposite the cemetery, where we

sheltered from the rain. She's facing up to the situation gallantly. You know perfectly well that she still loves him in spite of everything."

"Did she tell you that?"

"Yes. And she repeated two or three times that a man can't go on paying all his life, there comes a moment when he calls it quits. Edouard has reached the end of his tether."

"Is that why he's back?"

Although the tone was low, it was so aggressive that I couldn't help riposting:

"You seem to be forgetting about Christian charity . . ."

"Christ said: 'Woe to that man by whom the offense cometh . . .' "

"I know: 'If thine eye offend thee, pluck it out and cast it from thee.' But he didn't tell us to pluck out other people's eyes!"

Lucien looked at me in surprise, as if he had suddenly seen in me a man whom he didn't know. He said nothing, just gazed at the billiard table.

"Are you aware of the danger he represents?" he asked after a while.

"For whom?"

"To start with, for Philippe. It's all very well for him to have heard whatever people have told him about his father, but it's a very different matter to see him in the flesh, to watch his decline, to live beside him."

"Philippe is almost a man."

"As for Marie, she's managed to organize her existence

for better or for worse and her wounds have healed. What will happen in a month, in six months, in a year, when Edouard recovers? He won't remain in bed forever. He won't be prepared to live with her without doing anything. As soon as he's up you'll see that he'll want to look good, exhibit himself, elaborate fantastic plans."

"What can we do about it?"

I added ironically:

"Kill him? I admit that would be the best thing for everybody . . ."

"Shut up! What exactly did she tell you to ask me?"

"It's about you that he feels most guilty. So it's you who are supposed to bear the greatest grudge against him . . ."

My brother scared me because he was staring at me fixedly, as though it wasn't me he was looking at but Marie's husband.

"Go on . . ."

"If you made a gesture . . ."

"What gesture?"

His toneless voice seemed to come from very far away.

"Marie wonders whether you couldn't forgive him . . ."

I started to regret that I'd accepted this mission.

My brother retained his external impassivity. His hands were motionless on the table. Not a feature in his face moved. But I don't think I have ever before had such a sense of a man making an almost inhuman effort to control himself.

I perceived emotions of violence that I had never even suspected, and I was affected all the more because he managed to master them.

He had difficulty in articulating the words, as though his jaws refused to obey him.

"Did she really ask you that?"

I nodded.

"That I should shake his hand?"

I no longer dared look at him and I longed for the police inspector to come and interrupt us.

"So that on Saturday, as the oldest of the Huets, he can be chief mourner?"

I had thought of that that morning, too, and Marie hadn't dared contradict me. We all knew. None of us had any illusions. But Marie went on loving him. And it was Lucien who was being asked to make the greatest effort.

"Does he want to be at the funeral?"

"That's what I understood."

"Does Marie want him to be?"

I nodded again.

"Have you mentioned it to anyone else?"

"No."

"You haven't seen Mother? She doesn't know?"

"She doesn't know anything about it."

I sighed in spite of myself, as though the worst part were over. It was now up to Lucien and his conscience, Lucien and his faith. He was lucky enough to believe in God. Would that help him at a time like this?

We said nothing for almost five minutes. It was a

strange place to make such an important decision. But perhaps it was better to be in the presence of strangers.

I felt that Lucien was gradually relaxing in front of us. Finally, he groped in his pocket for his pipe and started filling it. When I looked up at him, his face seemed disintegrated. From white it had turned very red; his features seemed bloated, and his eyes bulged.

"I'll go and see her," he muttered at last.

I didn't need to ask him if he was going to see Edouard, too. Once he had agreed to go to Rue des Saules, he would go all the way.

I felt remorse. I had just inflicted torture on a man who was my brother, without even knowing in the name of what I was acting. I had discovered that a man whom I had always considered to be without problems and without temptations was vulnerable and, for a moment at least, capable of anything.

In self-defense he would hold these minutes we had spent together near the billiard table against me forever. It was all very well for me to be an intermediary, but it was I, not Marie, whom he would think of every time he remembered this emotional struggle.

As though it were possible to take his mind off it, I said:

"Incidentally, as I was passing by Quai Notre Dame this morning I saw that they were setting up a mortuary chapel."

He nodded vaguely.

"Is the body back in the house?"

"Yes."

"Who's watching over it?"

"There are two nuns. They'll take turns until the burial."

"Where is he?"

"In the little drawing room on the ground floor, the one that's not sealed."

"Did you go there?"

"At twelve."

"Was anyone else there?"

Even though the questions obviously annoyed him he answered them, and that was all I wanted.

"A few lawyers, some neighbors, some magistrates . . ."

"Did you have any trouble arranging for the funeral service?"

"Why do you make me talk?"

"Because you're taking care of all this! I don't even know what's happened to Colette."

"She's at home, with a day and a night nurse."

"In bed?"

"No. She roams about on the second floor. She had her dressmaker come and ordered some mourning clothes."

"And Floriau?"

"He spent yesterday night and part of this morning with her. Is that all you want to know? I've got to go back to the paper . . ."

He was about to get up when I held him back,

spontaneously because the words came to my lips quite naturally:

"Lucien!"

"Yes?"

"I love you. I'm happy you're my brother."

He looked at me, surprised, bewildered. He hadn't expected me to say that.

"Why do you say that?"

"Because that's what I think. For the first time, I really feel that I have a brother . . ."

He smiled awkwardly.

"Idiot!" he muttered, moved, and he held out his hand.

He added, as he was going to the door:

"I've got to finish the page setting . . ."

He greeted the police inspector on his way out, turned up the collar of his black, ill-fitting coat and walked across the street to disappear into the lobby of *Le Nouvelliste*.

I didn't have anything to do. Normal life would only resume properly the next day. The shops started to turn their lights on and the crowd on the sidewalk formed a disorderly procession covered by waves of umbrellas.

If I had known what movie Irène had gone to, I would have joined her there. I almost called her at home to hear if she had already left and, if not, arrange to meet her in town.

By some magic, for a few moments, I had just experienced a human contact, however furtive, and I would like to have preserved that warmth I had felt within me.

I was still seated at the table, alone, in a quiet café, before two billiard players who looked at me out of the corner of their eyes, and I finally signaled to the waiter to serve me another brandy.

I toyed with some riduculous plans for my afternoon, such as going to sit in my mother's kitchen for a moment, just to be with someone, to hear a voice talking to me. But my mother would have wormed everything out of me and God knows what would have happened.

Whom could I call on? Nobody! Nobody was expecting me. Wherever I went, people would have wondered what I wanted. It was raining too hard to walk through the streets looking at the shopwindows.

It was the town of my childhood, of my adolescence, where life was caged in on every side and where all one could do was to nurse one's boredom.

I ended up by going to Quai Notre Dame to "view" my uncle Antoine, whose enigmatic face was now surrounded by a frame of solemnity. I dipped the box twig into the holy water, traced a cross over the stiff body, and nodded to the two kneeling nuns.

I didn't notice François. I didn't dare go up to the second floor or ask to see my aunt.

When I came out into the street again, night had fallen and, holding my umbrella like a shield, I walked along past the houses.

Rather than go home, I preferred to sit in the darkness of a moviehouse, the first one I came across, perhaps the same one my wife was in. My shoes were drenched, and so were my trouser bottoms. My neighbor was sucking violet-flavored sweets and, in front of me, two lovers were sitting cheek to cheek.

I found myself laughing, mechanically, with the rest of the audience, because it was a funny film, and yet I was thinking that about that time Lucien would be arriving at Rue des Saules, his feet wet, too, and ringing Marie's bell.

All Souls' Day was Thursday. Uncle Antoine, who died on Tuesday evening, Halloween, was to be buried on Saturday. All that remained was Friday and it was a day like any other, with the town living its usual life, the shops open, the offices full of employees, the streetcars crammed, the market square in the morning bright with vegetables and fruit.

The wind had dropped, the rain was falling more sparsely and more slowly. In my mail, which never contains much, I found a summons from the notary Gauterat for the next afternoon at three o'clock and I couldn't help wondering whether that meant I was to be one of the heirs.

I've never inherited anything in my life. I have no idea what happens. Is all the Huet family automatically invited, whatever my uncle's last wishes, or does the notary only summon those who are going to receive something?

I would like to have known the answer but I didn't see anybody to ask. Would my mother be there, too? And Aunt Sophie, the mother of Edouard and Monique, who, at the age of seventy-nine, was almost blind? She lived on the edge of town, in the Grand-Vert district, beyond the last streetcar stop, and I hadn't seen her for at least five years. She received her husband's war pension, in addition to his pension as a former head clerk, and Monique brought her sweets from time to time.

I am not self-seeking, I swear, and it was not so much because of the will that I became increasingly excited as Saturday drew near. I felt in the same state of mind as I had as a child the day before a ceremony, a prize giving, the holidays, or Christmas.

My uncle Antoine's funeral took on an enormous importance in my eyes and I am sure that I was not the only one to feel as I did—that people were rushing about, holding secret meetings, that some were having a dress made, others a suit, while the older members of the family took their old mourning veils out of trunks and chests.

Irène and I hadn't seen the same movie the day before and my wife gave me an odd look when I said that I'd been to the movies, because she knows that's unlike me.

I wondered if she was worried about what would happen if I inherited part of the fortune. Did she think that I would want to have a life of my own, to walk out on her perhaps, divorce her, or leave her to Nicolas, who would find it all very awkward?

I'm probably wrong. These events—which are not so earthshaking after all, which happen every day, and which most families experience sooner or later—had made me hypersensitive and I let myself be influenced by various details to which I would have been indifferent at any other time.

I went to the Academy by streetcar, as usual, because I would never dare go there by car, and particularly not in a light-blue car. I gave my morning class, which consists largely in going from easel to easel and taking the charcoal from the hand of a student to emphasize a stroke, correct a shadow.

This all takes place in silence. There are two sorts of professors: those who like talking and joking in order to raise a smile or get a laugh, and those who say only a single word from time to time.

Out of shyness, out of fear of causing an uproar that I would be unable to control, I am of the latter kind and I am regarded as solemn. I am well aware that among themselves my students call me the solemn idiot.

That morning, for the first time, as I looked at the white-coated class making no sound except that of the charcoal grating on the granular paper, I imagined the possibility of a life that would no longer be regulated by professional routine; I saw the class as though I were never going to come back to it and, quite unexpectedly, instead of feeling a sense of deliverance, I was panic-stricken.

A few days earlier, I had still regarded my work as a drudgery, as a dreary, almost degrading task. It wasn't only the buildings of the Academy, the space assigned to me, and the faces of my pupils that aroused my resentment, but also the streetcar I took four times a day, the roads I saw flash by, the shops, the passers-by—the town in which I had felt myself a prisoner ever since my childhood.

But now, suddenly, there might be a chance of leaving. I didn't think of it as a probability, but for fun, as I might think about how I would spend my winnings after buying a lottery ticket.

Instead of pleasing me, it frightened me, and that Friday I suddenly realized that I belonged to my class at the Academy and to my town.

At twelve I found Irène already dressed, which is rare, and her coat hanging in the hall meant that she had just come back.

"I went to see your uncle," she told me. "I've been wanting to do that ever since yesterday. I didn't tell you about it because I was afraid you might say I shouldn't."

"Why would I have said you shouldn't?"

"I don't know. I've never seen a dead man. I don't know how these things work."

Unless I'm mistaken, Irène had only accompanied me twice to Quai Notre Dame. Not because my uncle didn't like her. On the contrary, I think she amused him. The occasion just never presented itself. One didn't go there for family visits, but each one singly to my uncle's study.

"How on earth could they live in that huge, sad house alone together? I now see why Colette almost went mad there. I would have gone completely mad."

"Whom did you see?"

"To start with, two nuns kneeling on prayer stools on

either side of the body, reciting their rosary. They didn't even look at me. A woman of about forty arrived with three children, two boys and a girl, and all four sprinkled the corpse with holy water. I forgot to do it. I did it on the way out so that the two nuns wouldn't think I didn't know how to behave."

"Is he in the coffin?"

"No. Just as I was leaving, they carried in a very heavy coffin covered with metal ornaments. It looked like silver. Do you think it is?"

"I shouldn't think so."

"What shall I do tomorrow?"

"Go straight to the cathedral and sit next to my aunts and my cousins in the first row."

"Who is the woman with the children?"

"Was she tall, fairly fat?"

"Yes."

"Then it's almost certainly one of Aunt Juliette's daughters. I don't know her husband's name. I only saw her once, years ago."

"Are you sure I don't have to wear a veil?"

"My mother and my aunts may wear one, but nòt the young women."

I spent the afternoon at the Academy and, once my classes were over, I went to tell the headmaster that I'd be absent the next day.

"I know! I know!" he said. "I'll be at the funeral myself. The church will be crowded."

For the first time he looked at me with a certain

respect, or at least with a kind of esteem, which he didn't usually display toward me.

I don't know what happened on Rue des Saules. Lucien didn't telephone me either the evening before or that morning, and I didn't dare call him. Marie didn't get in touch with me, either. The only way of hearing something would have been to go and see my mother, who certainly knew what was going on, but I preferred not to, for God knows how she would have reacted.

I heard nothing from Monique and her husband, nor, predictably, from Aunt Colette.

In short, it was as though everyone were making their preparations in private.

Nicolas was supposed to dine with us, as he did every Friday. My wife told me that he put it off, giving a business appointment as an excuse, which is tactful of him and rather surprised me.

Irène spent the evening letting out her black dress, which was too tight-fitting around her breasts for her to appear in at the cathedral, especially for a funeral.

"I suppose I can use a bit of make-up?"

"If you go about it discreetly."

I read. I turned on the radio, then the television, nervously, in a hurry to go to bed, get it over with, and reach the next day as quickly as possible. I took a long time going to sleep, as did Irène, to whom I unconsciously communicated my impatience.

In the morning, I cut myself shaving. The first thing I

did was look at the sky, which was still gray, but a whitish gray, with a slight luminosity. It was no longer raining. Footsteps resounded clearly on the sidewalk.

I behaved as though it was I who was the organizer of the ceremony and worrying about how it was going to come off. Of course that was far from being the case, but I was involuntarily sensitive to a lot of details, as though they concerned me personally.

"Are you leaving ahead of me?"

"Yes. The men have to be at the mortuary chapel for the last respects and the start of the funeral procession."

"How about Colette?"

"I don't know what she's going to do."

"Are you sure the women won't be going to the cemetery?"

"Not the female members of the family."

"And the others?"

"There may be some, of course. It appears that twenty cars have been ordered."

I left on foot, crossed the Botanical Garden, where, in order to justify its name, metal plaques have been stuck at the foot of the trees with the vernacular and Latin name of each species.

There were already clusters of people on Quai Notre Dame, some standing, others walking up and down and occasionally looking up at the windows of the house.

I didn't recognize a single face. I assume that they were mainly small fry who had known my uncle, as well as inquisitive bystanders.

I walked through the archway, up the marble steps, and, in the hall, saw my brother Lucien who was talking in a whisper to Floriau. They were both dressed in black from top to toe, like me, and I wonder why we looked cleaner shaven than on other days.

I glanced into the mortuary chapel. In addition to the two nuns, there were two men standing at the foot of the coffin, big, strapping men, and one of them had a thick mustache. Their hats in their hands, they watched our group with expressionless eyes.

They were Aunt Juliette's sons-in-law. Her son arrived slightly later and joined them, after shaking our hands without saying a word.

All day an independent clan would be formed by those three men, who were more plebeian, more thickset than ourselves, with their three stubborn faces that looked at us with mute disapproval.

Never before had the world of Aunt Juliette, the world of the Lemoines, proved so different from ours, and I never ceased to feel a latent hostility between the two branches of the family. In spite of their mother, they were not Huets. They felt it and stuck together in a solid front.

"It's time," murmured Floriau, glancing at his watch.

The master of ceremonies approached us at that moment to ask us to move into the mortuary chapel.

We were taking our places as best we could next to the hangings, at a little distance from the coffin, when I felt a shock. Edouard came in, slightly out of breath, dressed in black just like the rest of us, and, without a word, without a sign to the others, took his place closest to the door.

His suit and coat were well cut and, in spite of his thinness, in spite of the lines under his eyes, he was the best looking of the lot of us.

When we were young, we used to call him the musketeer. Now he had grown a thin mustache and he looked more than ever like a cross between d'Artagnan and Aramis.

People began to file past, greeting us discreetly as they went by, around the coffin, and out again onto the sidewalk. Floriau looked impatient and I understood why when I saw him walk out quickly and come back almost immediately with Colette, in deep mourning.

The only illumination came from the dancing flames of the candles, and the flowers, which were piled as far as the foot of the marble staircase, gave off an intoxicating smell.

Floriau had led my aunt to the foot of the coffin, where they stopped a little way back, and he stood next to her like her gentleman in waiting. I couldn't distinguish Colette's features through the veil, but the light of the candles occasionally put a glitter in her dark eyes.

Some signal must have been given outside, because now a slow procession started to file past us, among which we recognized some prominent citizens— the prefect, the mayor, the judge, some lawyers, some politicians . . .

Did they all notice that Edouard was there? Probably not. Yet it seemed to me that some of them, after giving him their hand without looking at him, drew themselves up with a start when they saw his face.

They shook my hand, too. The headmaster of the Academy shook it longer than the others.

That lasted half an hour and not once did my brother's eyes turn toward Edouard.

Just when the master of ceremonies was coming forward, followed by the bearers, we heard a sob. It was Colette. For an instant I thought she was going to press her face against Floriau's chest, but he took her carefully by the shoulders and led her out of the room.

Everything else took place in what seemed to me a slight disorder. We were manipulated like supernumerary actors. I was surprised by the daylight, by the cold outside. There were as many people on the sidewalk as if it were a patriotic rally. I automatically tried to stay next to my brother.

The coffin was put into the hearse, which was covered with flowers and wreaths, and I was propelled into the first row between Lucien and my cousin Edouard, who hadn't yet said a word to me and who, his nostrils contracted, stared straight ahead of him.

I am almost sure that I saw Marie among the spectators. It wouldn't have surprised me if, before going to church, she had come to make certain that all was well with her husband.

I looked for Philippe. I hadn't seen him in the house. Either by chance or by some mistake of the undertakers, he was with the Lemoine group, where he looked totally lost.

Was it on purpose that the Lemoines were put in the second row of the procession? Did they go there on their own accord, in order not to be side by side with us?

The hearse started to move forward slowly. A choirboy followed it, carrying a silver cross, then the priest bending over his prayer book.

We followed immediately afterward, Edouard, myself, my brother, and Floriau.

We had to walk only three hundred yards down the quiet Rue de l'Évêché to reach the cathedral. Although people had already rushed into the church in order to secure a seat, when I looked around I saw that the procession filled the entire street, thinning out at the far end, with more women and children.

There was another moment of confusion in the cathedral square. I was told to go up to the coffin, which was being eased out of the hearse, and I found myself between Edouard and one of Aunt Juliette's sons-in-law as a pallbearer. On the other side I saw only my brother, who was up in front; the other two were hidden by the coffin.

The pallbearers started forward and just as we were passing through the portal and saw the candles glistening in the choir, the powerful organ let loose.

If I had to describe my chief impressions that morning, I would speak of confusion, bewilderment, and depersonalization. From the moment I set foot in Quai Notre Dame I found myself, together with a few other members of the family, to be the object of attention of dozens, and then of hundreds of spectators, and it was as though I had to play a part at a moment's notice in a play of which I didn't know the words.

I'd been to the funeral of my father, of my uncle Fabien, of various neighbors and acquaintances, but these had been simple ceremonies, with no pomp, in which everybody knew what to do.

My memories of that morning are fragmentary, as though I had been lucid only intermittently.

We, the men, sat in the first row to the right of the aisle. Edouard was nearest to the coffin, then came I, my brother, Floriau, and finally the male Lemoines, while behind us were the local dignitaries—the prefect, the mayor, magistrates, the president of the bar, and others, all of whom had the Légion d'Honneur, at the very least. Most of them were the same age as my uncle Antoine.

The women were on the left of the aisle and I had to lean forward to see them. Colette wasn't there, but Aunt Juliette, my mother, and poor old Aunt Sophie, all submerged under their veils.

Only once during the service did I catch the eye of my wife, who was in the fifth or sixth place and who looked pointedly toward the veils of my aunts and the Lemoine daughters to reproach me for having kept her from wearing one.

Contrary to my expectations, there was no Mass for the

Dead and the choir of the Conservatoire began immediately a Requiem—by Fauré, if I am not mistaken—that I have often heard on the radio.

Several canons sat in their stalls and I counted six choirboys.

I didn't dare turn around. I think that the church was as full as it is for High Mass on Sunday, and one could hear people coughing and chairs creaking on the floor. At one point, when they started playing the *De Profundis*, a child burst into tears and one could hear in counterpoint the resonant steps of its mother taking it out.

Because of the crowd, no doubt, there was hardly any mystery. The emotion, or my emotion, at any rate, was vague and impersonal. It was more like despondency. I wondered what we were all doing there, following rites that we understood only up to a point, and it seemed to me natural that my uncle should have decided to leave.

I no longer tried to find a reason for what he had done. I thought neither of Colette nor of Floriau, whose lips automatically murmured the responses.

I was surprised when Edouard leaned toward me and whispered:

"Marie asked me to thank you."

We were so small, all of us, in the huge nave of the cathedral where men had been kneeling for five hundred years. There were so many people suffocating our little group that it seemed to me the family had faded away.

"Libera me," sang the priest in a quavering voice.

"I thank you, too," added Edouard.

The deacon passed with the collection while the choir started singing again and the smell of incense spread through the nave.

Then there was the long stampede to the door, the cars starting, voices, which I heard bursting out behind me in the broad daylight, saying something banal.

I was in the first car with my brother, Edouard, and Floriau. The Lemoine clan followed in the second, together with Philippe, who couldn't get away from them. There was no real conversation. It was Edouard who asked, trying to see how many cars were following us up the Corbessière hill:

"Who else is coming to the cemetery?"

Lucien answered him, and that at least was a form of contact:

"Only the family, some close friends, and a few members of the bar."

I saw the café where, two days earlier, I had had an upsetting conversation with Marie and I looked at my cousin Edouard in amazement, thinking of how much had happened in two days.

He no longer looked like a wreck, a tramp, a dog in search of shelter and a pittance. He sat bolt upright and his hollow cheekbones and bright eyes made him more glamorous than ever.

It was the family that seemed out of place and felt ill at ease at the cemetery. The others were friends of the dead man, his peers. They knew each other and conversed in undertones, leaving us the first places out of correctness.

We found the priest and a choirboy already standing by the tomb. It all seemed to me to happen very quickly and soon we were wandering in little groups toward the gate. Edouard was still with us. His son had joined him.

"Are we meeting at the notary's at three o'clock?" he asked.

"The car is waiting to drive us back . . ."

"Philippe and I will take the streetcar. We're going in the opposite direction."

I jumped on another streetcar, leaving the car to Lucien and Floriau, while Aunt Juliette's menfolk went to have a drink at the café before getting back into theirs.

It went very well, on the whole. There was no unpleasant incident.

"It all went very well, didn't it?"

These were the words with which my wife greeted me. She added:

"I was the only one without a veil in the first row."

"Marie didn't have one, either," I replied.

"But Monique did."

"What did the women do afterwards?"

"We were separated on the way out by masses of people we didn't know. Only Marie followed me. She told me that she'd be grateful to you all her life, then she went off to cook lunch. How about you?"

I didn't know what to answer. There was nothing to say. Nothing had happened. Wasn't that what I had wanted? Nevertheless, I had a feeling of emptiness. I was disappointed. We hadn't even had time to think about Uncle Antoine.

Only strangers had spoken about him, especially at the cemetery.

It was like a very elaborate clearance sale. It had taken place to the accompaniment of singing, drapery, canons, a whole show that was way out of proportion to ourselves.

My wife and I lunched by ourselves, served by Adèle. The day before, Irène had suggested that we meet in a restaurant in town and I objected that we might come across some other people who had been at the funeral.

"Nervous?" she asked me as we got up from table.

"Why?"

"Another hour and you'll know . . ."

She pretended to joke but I felt that the idea of the inheritance was tormenting her, that she had started (just as I had, unconsciously) to take the matter seriously.

"You can take the car. I'm not going out."

For almost an hour I was nervous, uneasy. Then, at ten to three, I kissed my wife and went down to get the car.

When I arrived at Quai Pasteur, I recognized Floriau's car in front of the notary's house. A clerk showed me into a front office and took my coat, which he hung next to some others.

"This way . . ."

The room was huge. Some colored panes, that covered half of each window, created a very odd light. A few women in mourning, their veils thrown back, were seated in silence, as if in a waiting room, and my mother nodded at me discreetly.

Aunt Sophie was there, sitting next to her son, Edouard, as well as Aunt Juliette with her sons and her two sons-in-law.

Only Lucien was missing and the notary looked at his watch irritably when he came in muttering apologies.

Had all those who were present been summoned? Had some come of their own accord? I could never find out. One of the clerks brought along some chairs. Maître Gauterat glanced at us, as if to count us, sat down, changed his spectacles, and cleared his voice.

"Ladies and gentlemen, we are about to read the will of the late Antoine Georges Sébastien Huet, who died in this town on October 31 and was buried this morning."

His principal clerk, standing next to him, handed him a sealed envelope. He broke the wax with a paper knife, took out two large typewritten sheets, and started to read them without appearing to take any notice of us.

It was very hot in the office and, what with the heat and the tension, everybody was flushed. Green files lined the walls up to the ceiling. The colored windowpanes threw strange yellow, blue, and red reflections onto them.

"*. . . and according to the promise made to my mother . . .*"

Only certain words rose above the murmur.

"*. . . I leave to the sons of my two brothers, Fabien and Clément . . .*"

We weren't quite sure that we had understood, and we

didn't dare move or look at one another. Each of us must
have chosen a point in space at which he stared, trying not
to betray his emotions.

"*. . . my movable and immovable goods consisting of . . .*"

My mother shuffled her feet. Aunt Sophie craned
toward her and I guessed that she was asking:

"What's he saying?"

Then there was mention of a life annuity for François,
of a legacy for Mademoiselle Jeanne Chambovet, spinster,
residing . . .

Formula succeeded formula, juridical term juridical
term, and, in the end, none of us knew exactly what my
uncle's last wishes were. When he had finished reading, the
notary looked at us over his glasses.

"Does anyone propose to dispute the will?"

Aunt Juliette broke the silence.

"Am I correct in thinking that the Huet nephews are
the heirs?"

"The sons of Fabien and Clément, in other
words . . ."

He leaned over his notes:

"Edouard, Blaise, and Lucien Huet."

"And how about me?"

"He leaves you his mother's jewelry as well as a certain
number of objects, which I have mentioned."

"And how about my sons, my daughters?"

"They do not appear in the will."

"Do you think that's fair?"

"Since there are no direct heirs, the devisor was entitled to dispose of his belongings as he pleased. If you wish, you can contest . . ."

Without letting him finish, she stood up. Her sons and sons-in-law stood up at the same time and followed her toward the door. There she stopped for a second, as if about to utter a curse, but, too indignant for speech, she preferred to leave.

My mother then asked in a shy voice:

"Doesn't poor Colette get anything?"

"I can reassure you about her. Your late brother-in-law made other arrangements for her a long time ago and she will receive a large income from an insurance company."

"It wouldn't have been fair . . ." commented my mother.

And Aunt Sophie, leaning toward her:

"Is Edouard inheriting? Is that sure?"

"Yes, Sophie, of course."

The old woman contentedly resumed her silent immobility.

"Has anybody got any questions?" repeated Maître Gauterat.

He was so dry and contemptuous that he seemed about to strike the desk with his paperknife and declare:

"Going! Going! Gone!"

We still didn't dare look at one another. We were embarrassed by what had happened to us, embarrassed about profiting from our uncle's death.

"I must now simply warn you that the legal formalities may take some time and that the sale of the building on Quai Notre Dame appears to be difficult. As far as I can judge, the assets, including the estimated value of the building, come to about a hundred and fifty million old francs. Two thirds will go in death duties and fees, and I should think that the sum to be shared between the three heirs will come, very roughly, to about forty million."

He said that condescendingly, not to say ironically. He seemed to want both to reassure us and to put us on our guard against excessive optimism.

My mother couldn't suppress a sigh of surprise and she immediately looked at Lucien as if to say:

"At last! I'm so happy for you!"

Floriau showed no reaction. I should think it must have been a shock for him to see his wife left out of the inheritance. My uncle Antoine obviously wanted to leave his property only to true Huets.

"Monsieur Edouard Huet, do you accept the inheritance according to the terms of the will I have just read out to you?"

Just as he might say "I swear" in a courtroom, my cousin answered:

"I accept."

"Will you sign here. Monsieur Blaise Huet . . ."

"I accept," I murmured, taking the pen in my turn.

"Monsieur Lucien Huet . . ."

My brother's ears were scarlet. He was so moved when he signed that I thought he was going to burst into tears.

"I shall keep you informed, gentlemen, and I shall summon you individually when the time comes."

We were led out, just as we had been led out of church that morning. We put on our hats and coats and found ourselves standing, in slight embarrassment, on the sidewalk.

"Get into my car, Mother," said Floriau, taking Aunt Sophie by the arm. "Monique is expecting you at home."

"Are you sure you aren't busy? Don't you think you ought to call on poor Colette?"

The family dispersed once more and all its members were about to resume their lives, more separately, more independently than ever before. I, too, had a car and I offered to drive my mother home.

"No, son. It's very kind of you, but I'd rather walk a bit with Lucien . . ."

I was alone with Edouard, who held out his hand in the dusk.

"Good-by . . ." he said. "And thanks again!"

I felt more tired than after a sleepless night, as empty as after a long railway journey. I switched on the engine, passed by Quai Notre Dame and saw lights in the windows on the second floor, a shadow moving behind the curtain, that of Colette or the nurse.

I found Irène playing the phonograph full blast. Without turning it off, she simply looked at me.

"Yes," I said simply.

"Very much?"

"About fifteen million old francs each. It'll take months."

"Who are the heirs?"

"Edouard, my brother, and I."

"Not the others?"

"No."

We could hardly hear each other, and it was only when the record ended that I murmured, taking off my jacket:

"It won't change much for us."

I was suddenly sad. I almost started crying. I've never understood my uncle's gesture so well.

Yesterday night I reread the pages I wrote last autumn and I was surprised by the importance I then attached to certain things. I thought I had lived memorable hours. I expected God knows what sort of changes in my life and those of others. What exactly did I hope for?

Nicolas dined with us last night. It was his day. I suspect it won't last very much longer, because Irène seems more and more irritated by everything he does, by everything he says. For three weeks she's been going out at unusual hours, early in the morning, for instance, and she who is so unsporting has ordered herself a golfing suit. I don't ask her any questions. I'll know soon enough.

The only difference in my life is that, when my wife isn't using it, I take the car to go to the Academy. Perhaps when the house has been sold—the public sale is scheduled for next week—I'll buy a car of my own, a standard model that won't attract much attention.

Lucien has bought an option on some land at Corbessière, just outside the town, where he proposes to build and where, as he says, his children will get some fresh air.

I often meet Edouard in town and see him in cafés. Nobody seems surprised any longer about his being back.

I saw my mother again only on New Year's Day, when I went to wish her a happy new year. Out of tact, I did not take Irène.

"Isn't your wife with you?" My mother pretended to be astonished.

Since I replied evasively, she murmured, without completing her sentence:

"I thought that now . . ."

She resents the fact that I inherited instead of her. But she's pleased that Lucien should now have a "slightly easier life."

"Do you know what has happened to Colette?"

"No."

"She's taken an ultramodern apartment not far from where you live, where she can see all the men she wants. It appears that Floriau goes there several times a week and that Monique is very upset about it."

If that was true, it isn't any more, because Colette has left for Nice, where she plans to live from now on.

The last time I saw Lucien was a week ago. I went alone to the Café Moderne. I saw him in a corner, sitting at a table with Edouard. They were having an animated conversation. Edouard signaled me to join them and my brother seemed embarrassed.

"What will you have?"

"Coffee," I said.

"Do you remember my plan to launch a newspaper? Well, it's about to come off. We were just discussing it, your brother and I. I've already got a printing plant in mind, a modern one to which we must simply add a rotary press."

I looked at Lucien, expecting a denial, but it didn't come.

Life goes on.

I spent only a few minutes with them, feeling myself superfluous, and after finishing my coffee I left them to their plans.

The street lights had just been turned on. I walked along Rue de la Cathédrale, then along Rue des Chartreux, looking at the same shopwindows I used to look at when I was sixteen.